The Last Fisherman

*A novel of the last Pope,
the antichrist and the end of the age*

Randy England

CONVENT
HILL
PUBLISHING
MEXICO, MISSOURI

The Last Fisherman

A novel of the last Pope, the antichrist and the end of the age

By Randy England

Published by:

Convent Hill Publishing
1913 Cherry Street
Mexico, Missouri
www.conventhill.com

ISBN 0-9673607-0-6

Printed in the United States of America
by United Graphics, Inc.

Acknowledgements

Thanks to all my friends and my family who took the time and trouble to read the manuscript of this book. Thank you for your time, wisdom and patient suggestions.

About the Author

Randy England is Assistant Prosecuting Attorney for Audrain County, Missouri, where he attends Saint Brendan Catholic Church and lives with his wife Carol and their four children.

He is a 1990 graduate of the University of Missouri School of Law. Former Managing Editor of the Missouri Law Review, he has written on the new age movement, pro-life picketing, euthanasia and other legal issues.

The Last Fisherman is his second book and first novel. He is also the author of *Unicorn in the Sanctuary: The Impact of the New Age on the Catholic Church* (TAN Books and Publishers, 1990).

E-mail Randy England at england@conventhill.com

Chapter One

And what rough beast, its hour come round at last,
Slouches towards Bethlehem to be born?

—*"The Second Coming" by W. B. Yeats*

River Bend, Illinois was old as Midwestern towns go. Here the Mississippi was wide and slow where the lower city met the riverbank. The town was thirty-thousand people and full of history. In 1837, River Bend gave the anti-slavery movement a popular martyr when a pro-slavery mob murdered abolitionist editor Elijah Lovejoy as he defended his printing press. Twenty-one years later, during the 1858 Illinois campaign for the U.S. Senate, Stephen Douglas debated his unsuccessful challenger, Abraham Lincoln, near the river's edge, not far from the site of Lovejoy's murder.

Aside from the bronze plaques and monuments in the parks and squares, the most obvious signs of history were the white horizontal marks on the downtown buildings. These days, it seemed, only the river made history. While the great Mississippi was no longer the center of economic and social life, the river would never consent to be ignored. If the sightseer would get close enough to those marks on the buildings, he might make out "Highwater '65" or "Great Flood, Aug '93."

The north part of River Bend sat atop tall limestone bluffs. From those bluffs one could look away downstream and see the St. Louis Gateway Arch through the haze twenty miles distant. Bishops had once made their home in River Bend and a few were still buried in a damp crypt beneath the Catholic church that still was called the Cathedral. River Bend was worn and sleepy. A wake up call was coming.

The great brick convent on Danforth Street was once home to nearly a hundred Catholic sisters, but the number was far fewer now and half of those were retired. Whether fifty or a hundred, the number of resident sisters seemed to make no difference here where the nuns made their home. Indeed, a visitor to the old building and shady grounds would hardly suspect that anyone lived there at all. At least that was the feeling that twelve-year old Larry Foley got when he stopped in day after day.

If any outsider could consider himself familiar with the old mansion, that would have been Larry. Six days a week, the tall sixth-grader would trudge across the meadow that separated the first half of his paper route from the second. It was always about the time Larry reached the convent's back steps that his paper bag would have lightened enough for him to enjoy the relief that only slowly displaced the ache in his shoulder caused by the overfilled paper bag.

Larry never lingered long inside the darkened hallway; just long enough to lay a single copy of the River Bend Telegraph on the desk in the closet-like room that served as the convent office. "A hundred nuns!" thought Larry on that Friday afternoon. He wondered how so many nuns could share a single newspaper. He knew a few of the black and white habited sisters, the ones who taught at the Cathedral school where he spent his weekdays, but he never saw them inside the convent.

He had always thought of the silent building and its high, wide and empty hallways as a holy place. Like a church, but not like Church. Things happened at Church. There was Mass and singing. Every week you could count on some kid throwing up in Church, usually on a classmate's raincoat. Afterward the janitor would get to work with his bucket of sawdust. How different was the convent. Nothing ever seemed to happen there at all.

This afternoon, however, one older nun moved slowly through the dim hallway and nodded pleasantly as Larry came in the back entrance. A moment later, he had completed his errand and was on his way out the front door, strangely refreshed by his minute away from the world. Something made Larry think of heaven as he blinked in the daylight. Did anything ever happen there? He hurried through the rest of his route. The papers had been dropped off early that day and there would be time to get up a ball game before supper.

The youngsters' makeshift playing field was a mowed area at one end of a twenty acre clearing on wooded lands owned by the convent. Between the convent and the field was an orchard. Where the orchard joined the field, at the crest of the hill that sloped down toward Danforth Street, there stood a man-made rock grotto. It was a shrine dedicated to Mary, the Mother of Jesus. Perfect for sledding in the winter, Convent Hill was steep enough and long enough to give a good ride, but not so long as to discourage the trudge back to the top. There was a chill in the air, but no snow on that late Friday afternoon.

Roger Ellis was all alone in the end zone and easily gathered in Steven's touchdown pass. It was nearing dinnertime and the sun was low over the fields. "Let's quit," said Larry Foley, who was the senior boy on the losing team. The eight boys began to walk together toward Convent Hill, except for Billy, who had yet to learn how to end a friendly neighborhood game gracefully.

Billy ran past Steven with Steven's football. Steven reached out for the ball and Billy spiked it straight into Steven's face. Billy was half Steven's size and knew if Steven caught him there would be a double payback. The other boys cheered the chase and watched as first Billy and then Steven disappeared below the crest of Convent hill. By the time Steven reached Danforth Street at the bottom of the hill, the faster Billy was far ahead and Steven was winded.

The other boys neared the top of the hill. They shouted for Steven to wait up, but he was angry. Steven walked home, not waiting for the other boys. The Zimmerman brothers were already due home, so they followed quickly behind Steven, while the other four boys walked more slowly across the field. It was Frank, Larry's little brother, who first noticed the difference in the light at the top of the hill.

"What is that, over there?" said Frank. He was pointing to his right to where the orchard met the top of Convent Hill. Frank started to run toward it. The luminescence, easily visible in the fading winter sunlight, could be seen just a few yards this side of the long-neglected outdoor shrine. The others saw it right away and ran also.

They stopped twenty feet from the spot and stood still, watching the source of the light. There they saw a woman, beautiful and young. She was unmoving at first. Then she turned her eyes toward the boys and raised a hand in greeting. She looked to be suspended in the air, for the boys had to look upward to see her face. But her posture suggested she was standing on firm but unseen ground. Her dress was purest white and seemed to be flowing in an otherworldly breeze, even though the wintry air on the hill was absolutely still. The boys watched the shining lady on Convent Hill for a minute or so, saying nothing.

Larry and Frank might have made a guess as to the identity of the lady. Both had been taught the stories of Our Lady of Lourdes and Fatima at school. It was Roger, however, whose family was Presbyterian, who spoke first.

"I think I know who she is," he said. "Don't you Catholics believe that Mary the mother of Jesus sometimes appears to people?"

"Yes," said Larry, remembering his lessons. He and Frank knelt before the lady.

Roger looked to the lady and spoke to her. "Who are you?"

The lady smiled at them and said, "You are chosen to tell all the world the message that I bring. There are troubles ahead. Dark times and great times are coming soon. But there is also a great hope for those times and I desire that the world should know of that hope. Your task is to receive it and pass it on to the world. Will you return to this place tomorrow at mid-afternoon?"

"Yes, lady," said Roger. Now all the boys were on their knees. And then, only minutes after the boys first saw the glow, the lady was gone.

The boys sat back on their heels. "I can't believe this is happening," said Larry. "What do we do now?"

"I don't know about you guys, but I'm coming back tomorrow," said Roger.

"Me too," said his younger brother Bobby.

"Do we tell our parents?" asked Larry.

"She said we should tell, didn't she?" said Roger.

"That's right. I think she would have told us if this was meant to be a secret," said Larry. "I think we should go home together and tell them." At once the four boys stood up and trotted down the hill and ran the half block to their homes.

"This isn't a joke, is it, Larry?" said his mother, Jean Foley. "Let's get your father and go see where this happened." The Ellis boys' father was not home yet, but Mrs. Ellis joined the group. The three adults followed the boys back to the hill and hiked to the top. They listened without comment as their sons went over the story there at the very spot where the lady had appeared.

It was Larry's father who broke the lingering silence that followed the unearthly tale: "There's nothing to do but come back tomorrow. We'll all come."

The hill was nearly dark and the families returned to their homes. It occurred to Jean Foley that some professional religious help might be in order, so she called Father Bertoldi at the old Cathedral and obtained his reluctant commitment to come to the house for lunch on Saturday. After dinner she called two other neighbors, one of whom would spend the evening and next morning spreading the story about what Jean Foley's dreadful boys were up to. More than a few were ready to believe the bizarre story, but most just assumed that this was what these neighborhood boys did when they tired of chopping down trees, digging holes and setting fires in the woods.

Despite the widespread skepticism among those who heard the tale second and third hand, more than a hundred neighbors and their children were on Convent Hill by 2:00 p.m. the next day. Steven came, but Billy—still afraid of getting his ears boxed—stayed away. The Zimmermans all came. Father Bertoldi, drawn by curiosity and duty, had stayed after lunch. Now he silently prayed that this would turn out to be nothing, for he was not sure what he would do if it were not. Jeff Henderson was a writer for the River Bend Telegraph. He lived directly across from Convent Hill, and noticing the crowd, joined it.

No one, however, had thought to notify the Mother Superior at the convent, but soon she and a contingent of sisters came out of the cloister to investigate the commotion on the far side of their orchard. After an hour of quiet visiting, the group grew silent and drew in closely to the spot where the four boys stood waiting. Then the lady appeared.

She was all light as before. The spectators first saw the boys kneel. As they looked to the place where the boys' eyes where fixed, some of them saw.

"Do you see the light?" said one sister. Yes. Yes. Everyone, it seemed, saw something.

"It's the Mother of God!" The voice was Father Bertoldi's and he was shocked to hear the words escape his own mouth. He knelt where he stood and crossed himself. A dozen others did the same. Some saw the lady. Others saw only the light. Some thought they felt a trembling in the earth. But only the boys heard her voice.

"Greetings my sons. Are you afraid?" said the lady.

"No, Lady," each said shaking their heads from side to side.

"She is speaking to them," whispered one watcher after another as a murmur rippled through the crowd. A series of "Ssshhhs" came back and all became quiet.

"I am here to teach you of things that must happen soon. I want you to spread my message to all the world. Do you understand?" The boys nodded.

"Long ago, my son came to you but you did not accept him. You spat on him and whipped him and killed him." The radiant lady was silent for a while.

"Soon, very soon, my son will come again to you. Already he is among you but is yet hidden, my children. This time you will recognize him, and follow him. I will tell you how you will know him. His hands are the hands of a healer. He will heal the sick and the injured, but it is not bodily hurts alone that he heals. He will heal hearts and nations. He will make us all one; one planet, one people, one faith. Will you spread this message, children?"

"Yes," said three of the boys.

"We're only kids," said Larry, "How can we spread this message? What if no one believes us?"

"They will believe because I will give a sign to prove you are sent by me. Tell them what I have said. In one week you must return to me at this place. I will give a sign for you and for all, so that they may believe."

At once the lady vanished. The gathered neighbors slowly closed in around the boys. They had not heard the lady but each had strongly felt her presence, and now waited to learn what the lady had said.

Father Bertoldi was the first to question the boys. "Can you tell us what the lady said to you?" Roger volunteered and gave the message exactly as the lady had told it.

"Did she say who she was?" asked the Mother Superior.

"No, Mother, only what Roger said. That's all," answered Larry who often saw the ageless nun alone in the convent office during his daily rounds. Larry had just about made up his mind that it was she that read the paper and she that told the others whatever it was that nuns might need to know.

Once it was clear that there was no further story to be gained from the boys, the group broke up and started down the hill toward their homes. They would certainly come back next Saturday.

"Who would have thought I would ever see the Blessed Virgin Mary!" a gray-haired woman said as she picked her way slowly down Convent Hill.

"I didn't see anything but a light in front of the boys," said a younger woman by her side. "How do you know it was her?"

The elder woman turned to her with a quizzical look and announced in a way meant to settle the question: "Because it looked like her, dear!"

✦ ✦ ✦

The week that followed was frantic with hurried preparations. Henderson had written a feature story on the boys and the lady. The Telegraph ran it on page one and the story quickly snowballed. The next day the St. Louis papers repeated the story and by Wednesday the area television stations had insured that virtually everyone would hear of the beautiful lady by Saturday.

The Mother Superior had not formed an opinion as to what had really happened on that Saturday, but she was practical enough to know that the weekend was coming and tremendous crowds with it. If it had been up to her she would have liked to slow things down; slow down enough to think through what was happening. If she could not moderate the rush of events she would at least try to prepare for it. There would be a need for lots of parking and she quickly realized that the best way to avoid having the convent grounds and gardens trampled would be to allow the cars to drive all the way in and let them park at the far end of the field.

Father Bertoldi, while he had been excited at first, was bothered by what he saw and heard. Phony apparitions had long been a scourge of the Church, spreading questionable doctrines and causing divisions among the people. Now he had this in his own backyard and he was the senior churchman on the scene. His own bishop lived far from River Bend and was treating the beautiful lady as nothing to get excited about. Bertoldi could not make him understand that people's reaction to the lady might provide a great deal to get excited about.

Father Bertoldi turned to an old friend and schoolmate, Michael Lindsay, the Cardinal Archbishop of St. Louis, Missouri. While the lady had not appeared within the boundaries of Lindsay's archdiocese, geography dictated that she might become his concern. Lindsay agreed with Bertoldi that the lady was worth watching, but he would not come to investigate personally.

"You are going to have the press there on Saturday and if I show up it will just throw gas on the fire," the Cardinal told him.

"I know that Michael," said the priest, "but I can use some help here."

"Here's what I will do. I will send Bishop Shea, my auxiliary. You will find him perfect for this assignment. He will be at the Cathedral rectory before noon Saturday."

Bishop Shea was the youngest bishop in the country. No one had been more surprised than he when, three years before, he was elevated as Lindsay's auxiliary in the archdiocese of St. Louis. Lindsay had first thought Shea a little rough and inexperienced, though he obviously had a gift in dealing with

people. The Cardinal quickly learned, however, to trust
Shea's judgment. If something needed a close look, Lindsay
knew he could do no better than to send his young auxiliary.
Bishop Shea was such an accurate observer, Lindsay eventually realized, because he wasted no thought upon himself.

Bishop Shea arrived at the rectory at mid-morning
Saturday to meet with Father Bertoldi, who lived alone in the
huge old rectory. Forty years before, three priests had staffed
this parish. Now Thomas Bertoldi was alone in shepherding
the still sizable church, even as his bishop continued to warn
that they must prepare for a day of "priestless" churches.
Bertoldi was faithful in praying for priestly vocations but he
would no longer allow his mind to linger on the subject. Such
thoughts, he found, were only a temptation to anger and uncharity.

"Priestless parishes!" Bertoldi had nearly howled
when the bishop had first raised the idea. "Rather than rub-
bing our heads over what we shall do when there are no
priests, ought we not be insuring that such a thing never
happens?" Bertoldi had frequently seen that look of personal
disapproval in the bishop's eyes that told him he had stepped
over the line, but this time the look was mixed with sympathy, as if the bishop knew he would never get through to this
quaint, round and simple priest. Tom Bertoldi understood,
held his tongue, and went home all the angrier for it.

He had been a priest for twenty-five years and had re-
cruited seven boys, now men, to the priesthood. Two more of
his young men were currently in the seminary and Bertoldi
had his eye on half a dozen promising boys at the Old Cathedral school. Even before the bishop started talking about
priestless "services," Father Bertoldi had recognized that he
must redouble his efforts. Some years earlier, the Holy See
had declared the use of female altar servers to be permissible.
The bishop, having for years permitted the impermissible,
wasted no time in decreeing that the permissible was now
mandatory. Despite his own private reluctance, Bertoldi obe-
diently incorporated the young ladies into the liturgical program. He truly loved every one of those altar girls—they

really did look like little angels, he had thought more than once—but he also saw his opportunities to work with his boys, his future priests, cut by more than half. The trouble was, his little angels seemed far more eager to serve at the altar. It wasn't that the boys were reluctant, just that with the girls and their mothers so avid, many of the boys were inclined to hang back rather than to shove in to preserve their places. No matter, Bertoldi decided, he would continue to make vocations a priority. What he could not understand— Bertoldi was not a proud man—was why every other priest should not duplicate what he considered his own mediocre record.

Father Bertoldi greeted the tall young bishop with the powerful build and quick smile and shook his hand as he invited Shea in from the cold. He did not have guests nearly so often as he liked. As usual, the balding Italian priest made up for it by serving more food.

Bertoldi told Shea everything he knew of the lady and explained that he had spoken with each of the four boys during the week. He assured Shea that the boys were absolutely sincere. And he reminded Shea that he had seen the lady himself. After lunch, the drive to Convent Hill from the Cathedral lasted barely five minutes.

As they drove onto the convent grounds Bishop Shea observed that the lady had picked a very practical location. It was close to the population center of St. Louis, yet the spacious field could accommodate thousands as well as provide an appealing rural setting. The driveway wound around behind the convent and turned to gravel as it ran along the south edge of the orchard beside the woods.

As the orchard opened into a large field, Bertoldi pointed to the old shrine to their right. Already the field in front of the shrine was filling with people. Some were picnicking on the ground despite the chilly weather. Some were kneeling and praying the rosary.

Bertoldi parked in a roped off area at the far end of the field and they walked back toward the gathering crowd.

Both were dressed plainly, but were still recognizable as priests. They avoided the area where the press seemed to be gathering. Many of his parishioners greeted Father Bertoldi, but no one knew, or paid much attention to, the bishop at his side.

After more than an hour, there was great excitement when the four boys came up Convent Hill with their families and many of their neighborhood friends. The boys had come to the field early that morning to see what preparations were being made, but on this trip they were not ready for what they saw as they neared the top of the hill. The crowd itself was out of sight beyond the crest of the hill, so approaching the shrine from the hill side was like coming into a theater from backstage.

Now there were many thousands; some later estimated ten thousand. The throng parted to admit the boys. They walked to the place where they had stood on the previous Saturday. Quickly the mass of people became silent. Many prayed. Others, including Father Bertoldi and Bishop Shea just watched and waited for the appointed time.

Finally, every eye watched as the four boys knelt. They looked upward to the place where the lady now showed herself. She had the same radiance, the same sense of presence and yet distance, as if she was in another place. The lady began to speak to the boys. She praised them for their apparent success in spreading her message.

"Thank you, Lady," said Roger.

"What is going on?" said someone close to the boys. "I don't see anything." Only a few who had not been there the week before could see the light, but most of those assembled did not. A wave of disappointment swept through the crowd. The excitement of those who *could* see only annoyed the majority who saw and heard nothing.

Father Bertoldi was one who did see the lady, just as he had seen her the week before. He turned to Bishop Shea. "Do you see her?" Bishop Shea did not answer at first and Bertoldi repeated the question.

"I am afraid that I do." Shea said to him, sounding as if he wished he had not.

The lady was still talking to the boys.

"Children, my message is the same as I have told you before. You must look to the man that is coming. He is truly my son and you will know him as a healer. All the world will follow him for there is no one like him. Long ago men killed my son. This time they will not kill him. Indeed, he is under my protection and no one can harm him. I want you to tell everyone what I have told you. Do you understand?"

"Yes, we do," said Larry, "but Lady, what is the sign you said you would give so that everyone would believe?"

The lady looked from one boy to the next. Each leaned forward as if to better hear her answer. No answer came. And then she was gone.

One hundred and fifty miles down the great river it was a slightly warmer Saturday afternoon. When the trembling began, few felt any fear at the realization that southeast Missouri was experiencing an earthquake. It had been many generations since a killer quake had hit the area, but a minor shaking every few years was common.

A few seconds later it became clear that this was not an ordinary tremor. Buildings began to moan and crack; furniture and fixtures tossed about. Windows broke in their frames and people rushed outdoors quickly as buildings began to be thrown down.

In the small cities and towns of the area the scenes were familiar; crushed lower stories of buildings, broken highways, then fires and later the wail of emergency vehicles and the newly homeless taking shelter in gymnasiums and churches.

In the countryside the earthquake could be seen as keenly as it was felt. The waves of earth came across the pastures like swells of the sea, higher and higher as they approached. The trees tilted as the waves passed, causing the tallest to interlock at their tops. Then the great trunks stood straight again as the crest of the wave passed beneath them.

The earth roared as if in a continuous explosion. When finally the earthen waves became too tall they would burst open, hurling soil and water, sand and coal high into the air.

On the river the tall waves rushed across the surface overturning boats and throwing them far inland on the opposite shore. Then the return of water carried trees, buildings and people back into the river. An island upstream disappeared entirely.

Property was damaged 200 miles away and the shocks were felt throughout the entire eastern half of the United States. On Convent Hill the crowds were grumbling as the show began to break up. They had not come here to be told what the supposed "lady" had to say. They came to see some wonder. Now, for most, it appeared there would be no wonder.

Then the first tremor came, gentler than those devastating the Missouri bootheel, but still the strongest quake these Midwesterners had ever felt. Even at that distance from the epicenter the movement could be seen. Trees swayed with the earth and stones fell from the old shrine a short distance from were the lady had appeared. Some people ran; others sat down rather than try to keep their balance. The shaking went on for a long time before it passed. No one was hurt.

"The sign!" shouted one person.

"The sign!" repeated another. But many, particularly those who had seen and heard nothing of the lady, were far from being convinced that a seemingly minor earthquake was proof of a supernatural vision.

"Look!" screamed one of the nuns nearest the boys. She pointed toward the four boys; actually past the boys to the place where the lady had been. As those who heard looked to the spot, the earth raised like a great boil. Six feet high, the boil split open with a clap, cutting a fissure in the ground thirty feet long. Watchers scattered where the end of the rift opened up at their feet. Immediately vents of steam began to blast from the crack and the scent of sulfur filled the air, as solid debris began to blow from the center of the fissure.

In every direction the crowd fled. A great rush of people ran wide around the growing fissure and then down Convent Hill, but most of the crowd, including Bertoldi and Shea, turned and ran back across the fields. Hundreds abandoned their cars when the fissure cut across the drive itself. It was the first time video cameras had been present at the very birth of a volcano.

By the next morning every news organization in the country was at the scene, having been diverted from their coverage of the great earthquake. Mere destruction could not compete with the story of an Illinois volcano, a beautiful lady and her urgent message for humanity.

By the time the boys were brought out for a press conference the next afternoon the River Bend volcano already rose 80 feet above the crown of Convent Hill. After repeating the lady's messages and answering questions about the lady herself, their parents took them inside. Notwithstanding the closing of Danforth Street that Sunday to all but the local residents, thousands parked wherever they might and hiked in for a close-up look at "The Lady," as the volcano was coming to be called.

That Sunday night the violent cauldron at the peak of The Lady's cone was the highest point in River Bend. That evening, the curious gathered on the St. Louis waterfront as if for a cold weather Fourth of July. Looking northward, they watched her fling fiery lava bombs high into the air. Arching outward, the liquid rock then exploded with molten redness on her shoulders. On Monday, Danforth Street was closed forever by the dull red river that streamed from Convent Hill.

In a month she had covered a square mile with ash and lava, and in a year, The Lady would be a half mile tall, River Bend would be no more, and the great Mississippi would be diverted to meet the Missouri river miles above their normal convergence. Even so, The Lady was praised because throughout the upheaval and ultimate evacuation, not a single life had been taken by her coming.

Chapter Two

Turning and turning in the widening gyre
The falcon cannot hear the falconer;
Things fall apart; the centre cannot hold;
Mere anarchy is loosed upon the world,
The blood-dimmed tide is loosed, and everywhere
The ceremony of innocence is drowned;

—*"The Second Coming" by W. B. Yeats*

Three years earlier:

The Third Lexington Annual Pro-Choice Banquet was set to begin with drinks and dinner starting at 6:30 p.m. Later would come speeches and remarks and awards to acknowledge those members of the community who had made their own special contributions to the cause. Outside at 6:15, John Daniels arrived and removed his freshly printed sign from the trunk of his car. The bearded young man moved quickly for one so sturdily built. His friends no longer called him Bear, but the name still fit.

John wanted to be certain that everyone understood how he felt about the traitor Wolfe. Mason Wolfe had been elected to the legislature with the endorsement of the state Right-to-Life committee. He had courted the right-to-lifers with words before the election. When the time for deeds came,

Wolfe still had the right words, but he never seemed to stir himself to any corresponding action during that first term. At the next election, Wolfe was challenged in the primary by a woman who had been arrested after chaining herself to an abortion clinic door. The committee endorsed Wolfe again, partly through inertia, but mostly because it was firmly committed to ignoring the radical pro-lifers.

This was an election year and Wolfe's star was rising as he aimed for congressional office. While he was not the first politician to switch sides in the abortion brawl, his blatant turnabout after the last election was made more bitter by his newborn enthusiasm for the abortion establishment. John reflected that Wolfe, as a pro-lifer, had never risen above room temperature, but now he was the fiery convert, and tonight, the honored guest.

"Evening, Kathy," John said as he greeted a familiar face from the Saturday morning picket line. And noticing Kathy's sign, he added, "I see you came to express your admiration for our old friend."

"Wouldn't miss it. Why does it have to be so cold?" John watched as more and more people arrived to express their disapproval of Mr. Wolfe and his new friends. Two elderly ladies carried signs reading "The Wolfe is at the Door." The text appeared over a devastatingly effective caricature of a very recognizable Mason Wolfe looking just like a wolf and leering hungrily into the window of a doctor's waiting room at two pregnant women. Some teenage girls stood around and talked among themselves. John didn't know if they were just spectators; or protesters at that awkward age where they were too embarrassed to take up a sign.

There were certainly plenty of generic pro-life signs available for empty hands. Such events were typically well supplied with professionally printed signs for the ardent but less artistic demonstrator. Pro-lifers could usually choose between the secular, more strident slogans and a gentler religious theme. A man with two young boys took up a pre-printed "Abortion is Murder" placard so that his sons could stand splendidly by the curb supporting either end of a banner that

John could not quite see. Something about Wolfebait or Wolf-
bane. While neither the banquet nor the protest had been
publicized through the local media, someone had alerted two
local TV stations. One camera was set up across the road.
Another was focusing on the kids with the banner as the very
young and very blonde reporter was asking the father a question.

"Don't you think this is a very cold night to bring out
children to something like this? Do they even know why they
are here?"

"I suggest you ask them why they are here. They volunteered to come," the man told her, smiling at the two boys.
The reporter moved in on the smaller boy with the camera in
tow.

"Why did you come here tonight?"

"All the people going inside tonight think it is OK for a
mother to kill her baby. And that's wrong." The reporter
seemed disappointed with the answer, which never made the
evening news.

The group had grown to more than a hundred. Some
ate burgers and tacos out of sacks as they milled about with
their signs. Two mechanics had obviously not had time to
change out of greasy overalls. Someone was trying to get everyone to spread out and keep moving, but it was after six-
thirty and everyone wanted to be by the street to see, and be
seen by, Wolfe as he drove in. The guests began to arrive and
each had to drive within two feet of the crowd that lined the
curb and the entrance to the banquet hall. John saw that
each guest reacted the same way. First, there was the quizzical look at the signs and the crowd; then the scowl of recognition and then a glance away as if someone had brought them
a side dish they hadn't ordered. "They weren't expecting this,"
he thought.

John thought the situation ironic: outside in the cold
were the pro-lifers, mostly conservative, but difficult to shoe-
horn into the Republican stereotype of privileged, compas-
sionless and self-interested bluebloods. They were families,
they were teenagers and blue-collar workers and an old man

in a wheelchair. They came in their pick-ups and mini-vans. Inside were the pro-abortion elite, the compassionate liberals, rich ladies in furs and facelifts. They came in Lincoln Town Cars and in limousines. John smiled smugly at that and kept a close watch so as not to miss Wolfe's arrival.

"Do you know that priest?" John asked Kathy, whom he knew to be a Catholic. He pointed to a tall, athletic, red-haired man whose Roman collar was obvious despite the overcoat he wore.

"No, the only priest I've ever seen on a picket is old Monsignor Wheeler and that's sure not him." John was looking hard at the big shouldered priest with the large head and thinking how hard it was to guess his age. "Thirty? Forty-five? No, younger." Someone shouted: "It's Wolfe, it's him" and John shook off his thought.

Mason Wolfe was seated in the front passenger seat. Every sign was raised and thrust toward the traitor. The black car slowed to make the turn into the lot, as if to give Wolfe the opportunity to savor each sign in its turn. He held his composure better than the guests that had preceded him through the gauntlet, although he could not hide his disapproval of the "Mason Wolfe *as* wolf" caricatures.

Whether by coincidence or plan, no one seemed to know, but just as Wolfe's car turned into the driveway entrance another car appeared, blocking the way and halting Wolfe's car half in the street and half straddling the sidewalk. To John's right he noticed the big priest positioned perfectly as if he were Wolfe's doorman, ready to help the traitor out. Wolfe himself was looking straight ahead, but something drew his head to the right and his eye met the gaze of the priest. And there he was held. Dread passed over his face and he was, at that instant, completely undone. The spell broke only when Wolfe's car jerked and then accelerated, the other car having repented its error and backed out of the way. The near camera caught the episode. Then by seeming telepathy, both news crews simultaneously determined that the outdoor show was over and quickly moved indoors to the banquet, apparently by prior invitation.

With Wolfe and the cameras gone, and the thermometer dropping, the crowd also adjourned. John found a soft spot in the sod by the drive and jammed his sign into the turf. There were morning classes to prepare for. The sign would inform the latecomers that John Daniels had been there.

The mini-van stopped in front of the old rectory next door to an even older church building. "Well, now that I've dragged you off to a protest," said the driver, "I suppose you've been radicalized beyond hope." The man's two boys had stowed their long banner behind the third seat and were too busy eating cheeseburgers to pay any attention to the adults.

"You know, Ben, it is one thing to give the annual pro-life homily each January, and it's another to have your picture taken at a political protest and find it the next day on page one."

"You have to understand how important it is for you to be there," said Ben. "You encourage us all just by showing up."

"I know. And I appreciate you inviting me along. I was about to say that a priest can easily become known for a lack of balance. I'd guess that one pro-life sermon a year would be considered a 'safe' number. That's not really something a pastor should think about, but I think that too many of us do. I'm probably more guilty than most when it comes to wanting to be liked and respected."

"I don't know about that; but you *are* different. Like when you booted the Dignity group from the Newman Center at the college. And how many times have you gone chin to chin with Sister Eckhardt?"

"Ha! Sister Mary Ellen. How could we go chin to chin? She's fifteen inches shorter than me! What you are saying is that nothing I did today could send my stock any lower at the Chancery Office. Thank you for reminding me. It is not my courage that gets me in trouble, my friend; it is my mouth."

"Your stock may be low with the dear sister and some other folks we won't mention, but the bishop is a good man and you are an asset to him and to the Church. Anyway, I wish we had more such mouths as yours. And if we do not, I do not believe we can win this fight without crashing first at the bottom."

"And what is the bottom?" asked the priest.

"I don't know, but the whole world seems like it is bent on killing itself. The Jews and Arabs are fighting again and a month ago an Iranian bomb came within thirty minutes of vaporizing Tel Aviv. We have as many abortions as ever in this country. Euthanasia is legal in every state. Now the Supreme Court has decided that children and incompetent adults cannot be denied their right to choose euthanasia just because they lack the mental capacity to choose for themselves. So somebody must exercise that choice for them. And these damned doctors. Excuse me, Father. These doctors don't even wait till they've killed you before they yank out your organs. It's murder Father!"

"Moloch eating his children," said the priest quietly, almost to himself.

"What?"

"G.K. Chesterton. We're like the ancient Phoenicians and Carthaginians, offering even the lives of our children to insure our material comforts. Unless we can wake ourselves and turn back to God, we can look ahead to even stranger, more startling, obscenities. We are walking in our sleep, and trying to wake ourselves with nightmares."

"Where will it end, do you think?"

"Good question. See you on Sunday, Ben. Good night boys, are you serving Mass this week?" asked Brendan Shea as he opened the door and stepped out.

"Yes, both of us. Nine o'clock. Good night Father."

Father Shea did not go into the rectory but made for the side entrance of his church. He finally found the right key and was soon in prayer before his Lord.

✠   ✠   ✠

By the time Brendan was seventeen years old he had disappointed nearly every person in the Kentucky town in which he had been born. The boy had always been a natural athlete and leader. He proved it by guiding both his high school football and basketball teams to championships in his senior year.

No one enjoyed young Brendan's success more than Dennis, his proud Irish father, and no one was more shocked when he announced before graduation that he would not be attending the State University on a full scholarship, but would instead be entering the seminary. Everyone, from his father to his coaches, his uncles to the local newspaper editor, as well as each of his friends, was confounded by his decision; everyone, that is, except his mother. His father was still raging from his son's announcement when Mary Shea came to the boy's rescue. She declared that she had silently prayed since before Brendan's birth that she would have a son and that son would become a priest. Dennis knew the woman too well to doubt her word and he knew the power of her prayers too well to doubt his son's vocation. "The world needs its first Irish pope," she asserted, "more than it needs another All-American."

At the time of his ordination, Brendan had been thought a mixed bag. With the exception of taking top grades in history, he had been firmly settled in the middle of his class. Naturally winsome and gregarious, Brendan had the gift of being intensely interested in whomever he was speaking with at any moment. Strangers, men or women, without exception, delighted in him at the first encounter. Once out of the academic setting, his common sense and ease among his fellow men set him apart from his old classmates, all the more remarkable since he never lacked for strong opinions. Brendan could be brash and unpredictable, but he was never unkind.

Father Brendan was incapable, nevertheless, of seeing himself in those terms and was usually so fastened on his God and His people that only a special effort would draw his attentions to his own problems. Tonight was different for him, however, and he was very much concentrated on his own state of mind. His experience at the demonstration, the discussion with Ben, and even the odd brush with state representative Wolfe had left him strangely empty. He thought of Ben's unanswered question: "Where will it end?" The question seemed to go with his own restlessness. Brendan had spent too many years in prayer to be surprised that God should seem so far away at precisely that moment when he most longed for His presence and comfort. That much kept him from despair, but still he was filled with questions and even a vague fear. Those were the times when he most appreciated the ancient prayers of the Church and the habits he had learned in the seminary. He finished Vespers and made it to the community room before the education committee meeting was over. It was after midnight when he returned to the sanctuary to complete his Office and his day.

Brendan Shea dropped his lunch plate and fork into the sink and was about to tell Mrs. Rennes he would be out for the afternoon when the doorbell rang at the rectory entrance. He was already at the door and opened it to find a short man, about thirty, wearing worn jeans and a dirty T-shirt, his angular face needing a shave. "How can I help you?"

"Are you the preacher?"

"I'm Father Shea."

"I'm passing through town and heard I might get some help here."

"Are you hungry?" the priest asked and stepped back, waving the nodding wayfarer in. "I just finished a corned beef sandwich myself. Does that sound good? I think there's some leftover tuna casserole in here too."

"The corned beef sounds great." He watched the priest working quickly and within two minutes the man was feeding on the first of two weighty sandwiches. Brendan turned a chair around, sat down in front of the man with his arms crossed on the seat back. He was smiling. He quietly watched the man, who, if he had not been completely absorbed in his meal, might have wondered at the way this priest just sat watching him happily with his chin on his hands.

"How about a soda?" he had started to offer when Mrs. Rennes interrupted him.

"Father Shea, phone call. I told them you were just on your way out, but it's some 'ambassador' or something."

"OK. I'll be right there. Mr. uh . . ." The man looked up, nodding his head with each chew, and raised a finger in the air until he eventually managed to swallow.

"Ralph Dozier," he finally allowed and promptly took another bite.

"Grab a bottle from the refrigerator, if you want. I'll be back in a few minutes." Father Shea stuck his head into the office on the way back to his study. "Mrs. Rennes, would you please check to see if Mr. Dozier needs anything else while I'm on the phone."

Mrs. Rennes did not much approve of Father Shea's habit of bringing dirty men with no job and bad teeth into the rectory. She remembered the first such drifter to come to the rectory door. The man said he needed some work to buy food and Father Shea had politely told him he had no work for him. Father walked into the office and sat down to some paperwork. A minute later he was back up, looking first out one window and then out the other. When he went back to the first window, Mrs. Rennes started toward the window herself and said, "For heaven's sake, what is it? The Second Coming?"

"Yes it is," he said, dropping the blinds and sprinting for the kitchen. When Mrs. Rennes finally looked out the window, Brendan Shea was trotting across the yard with a loaf of bread and a bottle of wine in his hands and a salami under one arm. He was hailing the man, who was sitting across the street in the shade. Since that first picnic lunch, Brendan Shea had not only fed every stray that came to the door, he habitually brought them inside. Mrs. Rennes had no problem with generosity, but she was a little more selective about the objects of her charity. And if she disapproved of Father Shea's luncheon guests, even less did she like waiting on loafers and criminals herself.

"Mr. Dozier, can I get you anything?"

"You wouldn't have a beer, would you?"

"No, we have water."

"Then I'll have a soda, I think it's in the fridge." Mrs. Rennes retrieved a bottle from the refrigerator and set it down at arm's length away from the man.

When Brendan Shea returned, Ralph was finishing the soda. Father Shea seemed distracted. Mrs. Rennes, curious about the phone call, looked in and noticed the customary flush was gone from Brendan's face. He seemed dazed for a moment and then he spoke.

"Mr. Dozier, I am sorry we didn't get a chance to talk, but I have to leave. Mrs. Rennes, it seems I'm to be a bishop."

Chapter Three

The best lack all conviction, while the worst
Are full of passionate intensity.

—*"The Second Coming" by W. B. Yeats*

John Daniels had learned that the annual convention of the Association of Abortion Services Providers would be held at the Kansas City Royal Regency Hotel in April. The Thanksgiving weekend was quickly finished and John prepared to leave behind his childhood home, his mother and his youngest brother in Lexington, Kentucky. He told friends and family he would work in Kansas City through the summer and then pick up his University studies there in the fall.

John was traveling light. His belongings would not fill his car, let alone a small, slightly furnished apartment in central Kansas City. His duffel bag contained clothes and a shaving kit. There was room for one good suit and two boxes of books. And the notebook computer. John's notebook was not new, but for his purposes, it did not have to be. It was his private file cabinet and his only secure communications link with the others.

The sun had been up an hour as he drove out into the Kentucky countryside, past the rolling white fences of prosperous horse farms. He suspected that he would never see any of it again. And the same sun had settled in the west before he finally fit the key into the lock in the door less than a mile from the Royal Regency.

John connected his notebook to the phone jack in the bedroom. He had arranged for the phone to be hooked up only two days before and half expected a dead line. "Thank you Lord," he smiled when his modem detected a dial tone. John brought up his mail program and typed:

```
Msg#:    17
Dec 04  19:05:25
From:    John
To:      Jimmy
Subj:    I made it.


Just arrived half hour ago. This place is
ideal! I can easily use a bike to get to
work from here. Once I have the job, that
is. I am going to the Royal first thing
tomorrow and check the quality of your
information on the food and beverage
department. With my good looks and
experience, I should be on board and have
a paycheck coming soon. <grin>  You know
how important it is for me to get hired
without having a known local prolifer and
malcontent like yourself having to make
introductions for me.

We have to meet as soon as Peter arrives.
I'll check back in tomorrow. And
remember, no voice calls and no
unencrypted mail. Time to sharpen my
sleeping skills. Good night, friend.
```

He dialed up Jimmy's number in nearby Lee's Summit and listened as the two computers whistled and hissed at each other in what they apparently considered communication.

It was Jimmy's idea to reactivate his old computer bulletin board system rather than use the Internet like every one else. The government had criminalized the use of any encryption software for which it had no "back door" key to break the encryption. It was a simple matter to filter the main internet trunks to keep tabs on enemies, but not even the government had the computing power to monitor every phone call over the telephone networks. John's software was not exactly legal since it pre-dated the law requiring a software key for easy reading by the government.

John quickly uploaded the message to Jimmy's system. Then he showered and let the water run long and hot. Sleep came effortlessly after a long first day. He would be up at 7:30 in the morning for a very important job interview.

There had been an earlier time, a time before John had turned from protest to violence, and though he still acknowledged that he had once been one of those lukewarm pro-lifers, he could scarcely remember how he had felt back then. Not that he thought there was anything wrong with peaceful protest, but only that it was too late for it. He had been a frequent picketer at local abortion clinics back when he could actually stand on the sidewalk with a sign and hand out literature. Twice, John remembered, a pregnant mother had been convinced to turn back at the last minute. But John knew how rare those were. Mostly though, the young woman would get out of the car with a friend—maybe the child's father. Then the clinic escorts would swarm around to shut out the discordant sounds and view of the protesters and she would be hurried inside.

Even though the rewards were seldom apparent, John had believed he was doing the right thing. Then the "Rescue" movement's latest incarnation came to town. John watched and admired the "rescuers" who put their bodies across the clinic doorways in Lexington. He watched and admired as they were arrested and tossed in the county jail. And he felt

guilty for only watching. Public tolerance of pro-life protest
had steadily eroded over past decades, chiefly as a result of
increasing violence directed at clinics and the abortionists
themselves. Then two abortionists were killed in the west,
one in her own front yard. The women's groups had been
shrieking for years that a massive conspiracy was afoot and
two killings—five hundred miles apart—on the same day
gave new life to the charges. The abortion establishment
went wild over the death of the woman especially.

Dr. Janet Nashua had recently been featured in a
weekly newsmagazine in which she described her abortion
practice as "riding the circuit" to provide "reproductive services" to women who would otherwise have no access to abortion. She started each day at 4:30 a.m. and drove to a different outlying city each day. On Thursdays she would fly to another state that had no abortionist since the last one had
been killed by a woman with a pistol.

The article showed Nashua at her million-dollar fortress home, surrounded with bulletproof glass and a security
system that even a bank could envy. Janet Nashua, her jaw
clamped tightly on a smoking black cheroot, struck a thoughtful, defiant pose for the camera. She would not quit what she
was doing. If she did not help poor women she was quoted,
then "who was left to defend them from anti-choice religious
zealots?"

"Aren't you afraid that you might become the target of
an assassin's bullet?" the writer had asked.

"I may not see the end of this just struggle," she had
answered prophetically, "but my place is helping my sisters
while I can."

The article was barely off the stands before Dr.
Nashua's companion found her dying in her front yard. The
driver's side door to her Blazer was open; the engine was
running. Nashua still held in her hands a sign that read,
"Beware of Baby Killer." Her body armor and the bulletproof
glass in the Blazer; her attached garage with the inside entrance and the semi-automatic pistol she kept in her purse
had been for nothing once she saw that sign. She was angry

when she died—shot through the neck with a high powered rifle—six steps from safety and damning her unknown killer.

That was the end of legal abortion demonstrations. The abortionists' spokeswomen cited the "anarchy in our streets" and called for a safe and legal silencing of public debate on the subject of abortion. Blaming the "domestic terrorism" on the "climate of violence" encouraged by abortion opponents, the editorials all called for a halt to the protests.

Old arguments for a more flexible Constitution were quickly resurrected. "Our U.S. Constitution—yes even the first amendment—is not a suicide pact," wrote one commentator. "Experience has taught us that those extremists who condemn a woman's right to choose are aiding and abetting violence, and anarchy is the result." That sentiment, unthinkable a generation before, soon became the sea of consensus in which everyone swam. Federal and state judges became even more disposed to grant injunctions against any protest—peaceful or otherwise—outside of clinics. Congress quickly amended the old Freedom of Access to Clinic Entrances Act to forbid any anti-abortion speech or demonstration within 500 feet of a building where abortions were performed or where any "abortion provider" lived or worked.

Congressman Mason Wolfe (D-Ky) sponsored the new legislation and defended its constitutionality saying "This legislation will have absolutely no ill affect on the decent and law-abiding citizens of this country. Only domestic terrorists and those who aid and encourage them are affected by these measures. Lawful, peaceful protests on issues of public interest remain inviolable. And I personally remain staunch in my support—and even reverence—for the first amendment." The federal courts, already accustomed to balancing all equations in favor of the constitutional right to abortion, agreed with IRS sanctions against any church whose leaders' "rhetoric" endangered the public welfare.

John had met Jimmy on the picket line. Jimmy was small and wirey, with a wild mop of curly black hair. A full-time college student, Jimmy's major was religious studies but his passion was anti-abortion protest. John and Jimmy had always shared the same revulsion for abortion. Both were firmly convinced it was an evil that God would not leave unpunished forever. Both genuinely believed in the humanity of the unborn child that died every time a woman kept her appointment. But John could never be like Jimmy.

Jimmy Anderson was a screamer. Whether shouting "MURDER!" or quoting scripture, Jimmy would be heard. And quote it he could. When Jimmy held forth on the sidewalk it was John the Baptist blazing: "You brood of vipers! Who warned you to flee from the coming wrath? The ax is already at the root of the tree."

Jimmy's arms would flail uncontrollably as he kicked gravel across the clinic lot with unabridged contempt. At the same time he would shout a warning: "His winnowing fork is in his hand, and he will clear his threshing floor, gathering his wheat into the barn, and burning up the chaff with unquenchable fire." John was certain that each of those women inside could hear Jimmy's "PLEASE DON'T KILL YOUR BABY!" even as her unborn child was forcibly removed. That was what Jimmy the screamer intended.

It was Jimmy who decided to protest anyway once the injunction against all clinic demonstrations was issued. And it was Jimmy who spent 30 days in jail for standing on the sidewalk with a sign. The judge originally sentenced him to thirty days and gave him probation. When the judge asked him if he would abide by the terms of his probation—which included a provision not to picket near the clinic—Jimmy promptly said: "I will not."

John had not been willing to stand against the court order with Jimmy. John and most of his fellow picketers had never caused any trouble at the Lexington clinic and now the day had arrived when John found that he might protest abortion all he wanted, as long as he did it at least two blocks down the road from the clinic.

John remembered that when the "rescuers" came to town they preached the slogan: "If you think abortion is murder, then act like it." With public protest now illegal, John despaired at the thought that his most passionate convictions had lost any outlet. All he believed in had been reduced to nothing but a toothless intellectual position. Jimmy had been in jail three weeks when John made the decision to "act like" abortion was murder. He succeeded only in cracking the glass in the clinic door and scorching a brick wall, but it was a start; and he did not get caught. From that day forward, John would follow that slogan to what seemed its logical conclusion. He and Jimmy the screamer would change everything.

When Jimmy was released, John took him to dinner the next evening. "You know about the clinic being burned?" John started out tentatively. He knew he would go to prison if the wrong person heard what he was about to say. "I did it. I'd given it a lot of thought."

"So have I, but I didn't think you would be the one. It's always the quiet ones, so they say in the papers." Jimmy was primed for this discussion in a way John had not expected. Playing the silent martyr in jail was not Jimmy's way. They talked until closing time and both laughed at how pitifully ineffective each had been in his first attempt to defy the laws of man. They resolved two things that night. First, that next time the stakes would be higher; and second, that they would not get caught, at least not until they had done what they set out to do.

Jimmy was ready to shoot an abortionist. He liked the style of the shooter in the Nashua incident, but John convinced him that job was like a trick football play that would have to be buried a few years before dusting it off again. "Besides, what good has shooting them done? The clinic opens back up as soon as the police line comes down. The abortionists are going to keep doing what they do. What else would they do? Half of them are incompetents who can't do anything else."

"There is a time for everything, even a time to kill." Jimmy argued. "You believe that, don't you? And you can't say that killer isn't out of business for good."

"OK. OK, they deserve the worst, and more important, we have a duty to stop them. I'd do it if I didn't think it would make matters worse. We need to consider something that could work better." John was thinking out loud, "Maybe we could kidnap one of them and hold the headlines for weeks. He wouldn't be doing any abortions tucked away in a basement somewhere. But where would we go from there?"

"Nowhere, John. We'd get caught and he would be some kind of hero. We need to be rid of him."

"Wait a minute, OK? You can't just execute the guy. Sure he deserves it, but I don't think we have the right to serve as judge and executioner. I mean, would we have the right to sneak up and kill someone just because we knew he had killed someone and deserved to die? In the Bible . . . ."

"You're right. You're right, but you don't kill the killer for what he did yesterday. You shoot him for what he's about to do today. That's justifiable and you know it."

"No, I don't." John countered, "If we assume we are justified in stopping him from killing again today—and I agree that we are—we are not justified in doing any more than it takes to stop him. Like I said, kidnap him. Look, Jimmy, if you've got a shotgun and he gets out of his car at work, you don't have to blow his head off. Why don't you just blow his hands off! That ought to be enough to get him into career counseling." John stopped a moment, then continued, "And if he needs his hands to do abortions, he also needs a place to do them."

"We could shut down the clinic again, like you did when I was in jail. What did it take, John, ten minutes to sweep up the glass?" Jimmy joked. "Actually, I know a guy you should meet. His name is Peter Hancock. He knows about this stuff and he wanted me to help him before I went to jail. I wasn't ready then. But I am now."

Jimmy arranged a meeting for the next afternoon and the three men met for the first time. Peter was cordial, but reserved. At first glance, Peter's sun-bleached hair and prematurely weathered face gave him the look of an aging surfer bum, a man without a care, but he was not what he seemed. Peter was the most serious man John had ever met. Now he was serious about hitting the abortion establishment. Peter was older than John or Jimmy, a thoughtful planner, selective and narrowly focused. And he was apparently rich. Peter explained that when his grandfather died, the old fellow had wisely left trust funds set up for his several grandchildren. As is customary, the beneficiaries could not get control of the money until they had reached a considerably more responsible age than 18. "How was granddad to know," Peter told them, "that I wouldn't do anything really crazy until I was over thirty!"

When Peter revealed just how available things like weapons and explosives were if you had funds and knew the right people, John started speculating as to how to get a bomb inside a clinic. John had experienced that difficulty first hand and knew that the problem had only gotten worse as security tightened around the clinics.

"That's already figured out," said Peter, "although they will close off my solution as soon as they catch on. Obviously, you can't get anywhere throwing things or setting something off outside. You've got to get inside. Steel doors you know; no windows; and they've got burglar alarms. And you can't cut your way in. We are never going to get away with firing up a 60 pound, gas-powered metal saw at the back door. Too noisy. I know that because I was nearly caught doing it once. After that I started thinking: OK, what's unprotected, here? Well, the roof."

"The vents, right?" Jimmy jumped in.

"Very good. Now I thought you could lower some sticks of explosives down the hole, light a ten-minute fuse and clear out. That might tear things up a bit. But, I'm thinking; I don't just want to tear things up, I want to shut the place down for good, right? So go back to the vent pipe. What is that thing? Two inches across? Four? Six inches across?" Peter drew a side view of a building and sketched in a vertical vent pipe. He added a little commode at the bottom for fun. "We use that vent like a mining borehole. Doesn't actually have to be a plumbing vent. Could be restroom exhaust or something, although I'd rather not chance using anything with heat coming out of it. Anyway, instead of dropping a few sticks of dynamite down the hole, the same hole serves as the casing for the equivalent of a stick four inches thick and twelve feet long. I can get high explosives in a pourable form, so we just haul the boxes up there and pour it down the vent."

"Boom, no clinic. I wouldn't want to be sitting on that pot!" Jimmy said and then whistled under his breath. "Man, I'm excited." John was excited too.

It fell to John and Jimmy to pick the targets, while Peter set about obtaining the materials they would need for the first job. They would not go to any nearby clinic where they might be known. They would select three possible targets to attack in one night, in hopes that two would prove workable. Each would be a single story building likely to have some roof vent and low enough that access to the roof could be had.

As a practical matter the timing required that one night's work consist of two targets in one city and the third within a two or three hour drive. No doubt the explosion at one clinic would raise an alert at any other clinic in the same area. Jimmy and John went first to Cincinnati, then Indianapolis and St. Louis checking the layout of every abortion clinic in each city as well as those in smaller towns in between. They noted any sheltered areas where access might be gained to the roof. What they found was that most clinics had no areas sheltered from view. On the other hand, if a man crouched low on many flat roofs he would not be seen from the ground. They were surprised to find how many clinics employed 24-hour security guards.

At each site John and Jimmy diagrammed the neighborhood, exit routes, lookout points and the best approach to the roof of each clinic. They had to forego knowing the layout of each rooftop. If the roof were visible from any nearby vantagepoint, then likewise would they be visible when they got up there. John obtained the police radio frequencies in each area. Nothing was to be written down on paper. "I don't intend to get caught with the equivalent of a confession in my pocket," said John. "We can work this so that unless we are caught in the act itself we will never be tied to the bombings." John recorded every detail on his notebook computer. He explained to Jimmy how they could safeguard all the information they gathered. "Once I've saved the computer file, I run it through an encryption program so nobody can read it without the password."

"But can't they decode it?" wondered Jimmy.

"Well theoretically yes, but it would not be easy. One of the ways to attack an encrypted file is to look for repeating patterns of characters. The frequency and positioning of characters in English have been carefully studied and a good deal can be learned by comparing a file's contents with statistical profiles. One way to slow down that tactic is to compress the file before encrypting it. Compression removes the natural redundancy in those repeating letters and patterns."

"OK, but can't they just keep trying passwords until they hit the right one?" Jimmy asked.

"Sure, but let's assume you had a computer program that could try each of the many trillions of 10-letter passwords, one after the other. A fast PC would be obsolete before it hit on just the right combination. I'll use a sixty-letter password. It's really pretty good protection considering that I put thousands of data files on this thing and every one is encrypted. I've also tinkered with a lot of the file dates so that even if you brought in the FBI to work on this thing they wouldn't have a clue which ones to start with."

"They shall be ashamed and also confounded, all of them: they shall go to confusion," Jimmy recited.

"What?"

"Isaiah 45:16. And of course you delete each one as we finish with it," he added.

"Not just delete," John continued. "The moment we don't need the file any more I will do a complete wipe and it will be irretrievable by anyone."

Peter bought the explosives but avoided saying specifically where they came from. Peter would only allow that there were thousands of people in perfect agreement with their methods and many in a position to help. Apparently so, John thought. Their mission required little else beyond the explosives. Flashlights and gloves, a walkie-talkie, radio scanner and the computer would make the trip. And a homemade rope ladder to use, and then leave behind at each bombing.

It was just after midnight when they passed the city limits sign of the south St. Louis suburb. John was driving as they passed the Women's Health Center. The clinic sat in a silent wooded office park.

"Well at least we'll have plenty of light to work by." Peter remarked sarcastically, referring to the sports park-style illumination all around the building.

"Just wait till we get around the side of it." John reminded him as they passed the clinic. "OK, look. There's no buildings on this side, just trees. You go up right there on the far side. Only someone on this road could see you going up, and then only if they were coming from the other way. There is no guard, at least there was not the last time we were here."

John pulled into the apartment complex on the same side of the road as the clinic. Jimmy and Peter would walk to the target through two hundred feet of woods as John watched and listened in the car from his position in the parking lot. From his spot by the road he could not see the Women's Health Center, because of the woods that separated it from the apartments. He could see a half-mile of road in either direction, which meant he could give the others nearly a minute's warning before any vehicle would pass by.

"Jimmy, I think a short prayer would be in order," John suggested.

Jimmy asked for success in a righteous cause, including a plea that no innocent person, present company included, should come to harm. As Jimmy reached for the door handle he finished the prayer with the words of Christ: "I have come to bring fire on the earth, and how I wish it were already kindled."

"Well, I've got the matches," added Peter, "so let's get to it."

Peter and Jimmy got out and went straight to the trunk. The explosives were divided between two backpacks.

Jimmy took the walkie-talkie, plugged in the earphone and put it in his ear. John keyed the mike on his CB radio and Jimmy nodded that it was working. They all hoped they would not need it. Peter carried the ladder that he would hook over the edge of the roof.

The woods were not overgrown and they hiked through the trees in two minutes. No lights appeared. John glanced down at the police scanner as it raced through 100 channels every second. Only a dozen channels were of any importance to the night's events and John had locked out most of the others. None of the radio traffic appeared interesting.

Peter got the ladder hooked over the roof's edge on the second throw and went straight up as Jimmy held the bottom. The scanner stopped on an odd channel. John glanced at the readout and thought, "Not one of the police frequencies." Then he heard a dial tone followed by three pulses.

"911, What's your emergency?" came the first voice.

"There is a suspicious car parked outside my apartment and a man is sitting in it," said another voice, upset and obviously that of the caller.

"Cordless phone call," was John's immediate reaction. He was amazed what people would say over those things even though anybody within a block could be listening. He didn't need to hear more to know that she was nearby and the only suspicious car with a man in it was the one he was sitting in. But it got worse.

"Two men got out of the car, put on backpacks and went into the woods. Something's going on." The conspirators had worked out a quick code to communicate. Various signals were worked out regarding pickup schemes. "One" meant trouble: get out immediately.

John grabbed the microphone at once and keyed it saying "One, one." He waited a moment and repeated "one."

Jimmy spoke up the ladder, "Peter. Peter." Peter looked back. "John says one."

"I can't believe this, how on earth . . . ." but he stopped and shrugged and picked up the pack he had just set down and hung the fifty pound pack down low enough for Jimmy to catch. Jimmy drew back. "Don't worry. You've got the dangerous stuff. This one won't go off." Peter dropped the pack into Jimmy's outstretched arms. Peter dislodged the ladder and threw it down from the roof. Then he eased himself over the edge, dropped down and rolled on the grass.

"Do you see any one coming?" said Peter rebounding and gathering up the ladder.

"No, John was supposed to be right here in one minute and it's been a minute. Wait, there's headlights."

"Well that's John or we're dead ducks, let's get out there!" said Peter grabbing up the pack. It was John.

Peter and Jimmy readied to jump in the car on either side and John stopped quickly and immediately jumped out demanding, "The trunk, put it all in the trunk." and he popped the lid. Seconds later they were moving and headed away from both the clinic and the neighborhood watcher on the cordless telephone. John explained as he kept to the speed limit.

"She was sure something big was up and she's going: 'Well I'm standing right here looking at him outside my window!' and I looked around and there she was at the second floor window. Thank God she knew nothing about automobiles. All she could tell the dispatcher was that this car was white and she was wrong about that."

John looked in the rearview mirror and wanted to curse at the sight of flashing emergency lights. "Look back," he said, and they all knew what John knew.

"When he stops us you know the story. He'll try to separate us and catch us in a lie," Peter reminded them. "Good thing you remembered to make us use the trunk. If this cop wants to search the answer is no. Got that? NO! He'll have no reason to search and he can't get into the trunk unless we let him. Agreed?"

"He's turning," shouted John.

"What?" said Jimmy and Peter as they both jerked back around to the rear. Together they sighed as the lights turned into the driveway of the apartment complex.

"If I had waited to hear the call go out from the dispatcher, we'd have been sitting out in front of the clinic dumping packs in the trunk when that patrol car showed up. Well, what now?"

"I vote to go north and hit number two." said Jimmy, talking about Family Planners, a clinic notorious in the region for doing late term abortions.

"Peter," said John, "What do you think?"

"Columbia."

"I agree," answered John. "The cops are going to be looking around a bit and they may suspect what was going on, what with the eyeful that neighborhood watcher got."

The scanner crackled and they heard, "I'm contacting the subject. Let's have 851 check up at Women's Health. 10-4, got that, I'll be there in a minute."

"I change my vote, let's go to Columbia," Jimmy answered in response to the scanner. The car passed the city limit sign and into the next colored patch on the St. Louis map. Five minutes later they were on the I-270 loop headed north to I-70 west.

The plan had been to blow up the first clinic and then take I-70 west to Kingdom City, Missouri where Peter's car— and the next set of explosives—waited at a 24-hour truck stop.

"Well, you guys are the experts on the Columbia clinic," said Peter. "We've got half again as much explosives as Jimmy and I can easily carry. Keep in mind that the key to pulling this off is making sure that nothing is left to tie us to the bombing when we are through. The only way to do that is to haul the extra explosives up to the roof and send it up with the rest."

"I think we can do it all at Columbia," John said as he pulled to the shoulder and hurried around to the passenger side. "Jimmy, you drive. I want to recheck the Columbia layout," he said as he popped the top of his notebook and waited as the computer booted up. He located the trip file and ran the decryption program. At the <password> prompt John remembered the psalm as he typed: "columbia mo the lord is my shepherd i shall not want." The computer worked a bit and spit out the unencrypted file. John brought up his notes and map on the word processor and read aloud.

"Columbia is the best target we looked at. The clinic is on a main thoroughfare, but it's also on the corner of a rather dark residential street. The entrance is on one end of the building, but the backside is isolated and invisible from the street. There is even a dumpster enclosure in back so you can hide if need be and even climb up to the roof without a ladder. I can sit just down the street at either of two all-night convenience stores and see everything coming in both directions. And the place has a raised façade so high that you and Jimmy would have to stand on tiptoes to be seen once you are on the roof."

"This place must have led a charmed existence, with no better security than that," observed Peter.

"It's a University town and a pro-abortion island in the middle of a much more conservative state," Jimmy said. "The 'Rescue' movement in Columbia lasted about ten minutes."

"Anyway," John continued, "I think we can get everything onto the Columbia clinic easily. We have lots of time. Let's pick up all the stuff at your car, Peter, and get on with it."

It was 2:20 that morning when they made it to the Kingdom City exit. Columbia and "Reproductive Services" were another twenty miles down the road when they pulled up next to Peter's car at the truck stop north of the highway. The place was busy enough that they drew no attention to themselves as Jimmy shuffled two boxes from Peter's into John's car and double-checked to see that nothing was left behind.

Peter moved his car to the competing restaurant across the highway and waited while John took a couple minutes to reset the scanner to receive the Columbia Police frequencies. "Everything ready? Let's go find Peter." Peter had walked from where he had parked his car and John and Jimmy picked him up at the front corner of the restaurant. John turned west down the ramp to the interstate. Jimmy was quiet. Peter reviewed the computer file one last time. "Are you done with this file?" he asked John.

"Well let's keep the encrypted one, but yeah, when you're done, do a wipe on the unencrypted file you're looking over now. Just highlight the file you want to delete and click the *Wipe* button." Peter settled all the details in his mind, easier now that he could forget the setup at the St. Louis clinics.

"Anything you want to see before I shut the computer off, Jimmy?"

"No, I've got it," Jimmy answered. Peter finished up and shut the machine down as they passed the first Columbia exit and began looking for the Fortune Road Exit. A mile further on, John signaled and left the interstate and turned north toward Reproductive Services. Three blocks later they slowed as they entered a brightly lit intersection populated with two all night convenience stores and a restaurant. John pulled into a parking lot.

"Do you think you can hang out at this corner for thirty minutes without alarming the local citizens?" Peter kidded John.

"No lurking for me this time. I'll kill the time on that pay phone over there," observed John. "I can't see any better place for watching up and down the street. What better excuse to sit in one spot than to be yappin' on the phone?"

They re-entered Fortune Road and went one block further north, passing the clinic on the left. John turned left on the residential street beside the clinic and drove slowly down its full length. It was quiet and dark except for liberally spaced street lamps. They circled the block once and John drove into a small, darkened park, which six hours before had accommodated two loud youth league teams and the normal complement of parents and friends. The charge of the lights and noise was long dissipated as the three men emerged from the car. Peter and Jimmy had decided they would carry a double load rather than risk a second trip for the rest of the explosives. It was less than a block to the clinic. John would drive up to the corner and give a coded "all clear" from Fortune Road. They could see the full length of the side street and, if they hustled with their load, could be at the clinic in half a minute. The signal came and they set off.

A minute later they dropped to their knees, exhausted and with hearts pounding. The experience at Women's Health had told them that it was pointless to stroll nonchalantly with a suspicious load on one's back. The other option was to get to the target as fast as possible and that is what they did. Jimmy and Peter moved everything into the dumpster enclosure, which seemed an enormously stupid addition to a building that was certainly a potential target.

"That was fun," Jimmy puffed, "especially since we decided we had to drag everything, including the second rope ladder, to this stinking place."

"It was either bring it with us or drop it in the trash somewhere else where someone might have seen us. The last thing we . . . ."

"Wait a second," said Jimmy as the radio clicked in his ear. Then he heard John's voice warning "Four." and then a few seconds later, "Four."

"Police car coming by," he said. Peter pulled the dumpster gate shut. They heard the patrol car pull into the front side of the building and listened to its sound grow louder as it came around even with the back of the building. It stopped, engine running. Jimmy held his breath when he saw a light playing along the top of the enclosure and along the back of the clinic. Squeezed like this, between a giant garbage can and a short wall, there was nothing to do but wait and see if they had been discovered. He shut his eyes and prayed, waited and prayed some more. Finally the sound of the engine departed.

"He's gone," said Peter, "and he went back to the main road. Routine check. If anyone had reported us he would have gone down the street the same direction we came from. Nobody's seen us. I'd bet he won't be back until we are long gone. Let's get up there." Peter climbed on top of the dumpster wall and after securing the ladder over the roof's edge, he swiftly scaled the wall. Jimmy heaved up both packs and climbed up after Peter.

Peter was already scouting the flat, tarred roof, which sprouted several promising conduits. He found the plumbing vent he expected to find but was attracted to a larger taller vent. "Look at this," Peter said, signaling for Jimmy to come to the spot. Peter pushed the vent sideways. Then seizing one side he motioned for Jimmy to grab the other. Rocking the tall pipe back and forth, the tube broke free an inch or so below the roof level. "You know what this is, don't you?"

"A furnace vent or something?" answered Jimmy.

"Something is right! These guys have got an interior fireplace or stove. This vent must be eight inches across and that means we can get every ounce of the explosives inside the building." Peter was shining his flashlight down the flue in the roof and could see that the hole was about ten feet deep and seemed to end at about ground level. "No heat coming out. Really, this is perfect."

Jimmy could only watch as Peter began to work. As Peter had explained it to him, the primer cord would ignite the main explosive, which would be poured down the flue. The cord, which looked to Jimmy like clothesline, was ignited by a blasting cap and the blasting cap by a burning fuse. Peter had prepared each of two sticks of dynamite with an oblique hole through its center. To give the whole thing a boost, he threaded the primer cord through the first stick and then the second, leaving the lower stick dangling about two feet from the bottom end of the cord. The second he adjusted so it would hang about four feet up the cord from the first stick. "OK, shine the light down the hole for me." Peter slowly let the primer cord down the flue until the end of the cord bent on contact with the bottom and then he gave Jimmy the cord to hold. Peter pulled open the packs and removed a 50 pound cardboard case from each one. He poured the first box down the flue, stopping to check the position of the primer. He was satisfied and quickly hefted the second box, pouring it down the hole after the first. Jimmy could see that both sticks of dynamite were covered by the pourable explosive. "That's it, a hundred pounds right where it will do the most good," Peter said.

John had just hung up the pay phone and was about to make a second pretend call when he saw the same Columbia Police Department patrol car turn north up Fortune Road toward the clinic. He debated giving the warning. What if the same cop had heard the first code "Four?" He stuck to the plan except he gave just one warning: "Four." It was enough. Peter and Jimmy lay down flat and waited. The patrol was the same as it was fifteen minutes before. The car rolled through the front, then around back. Jimmy watched the spotlight as it caught the edge of the roof in back.

"No wonder they haven't hired a private security guard here," he thought. "They get the same service for nothing from the police." It was soon quiet again and Peter resumed working. He cut off the primer cord and used friction tape to attach the blasting cap and safety fuse he had prepared earlier.

"How much time would you like before this thing goes off?" asked Peter. "We can go 30 minutes on this fuse if we want."

"The longer the better, but how about using the second fuse and cap as insurance against something going wrong with the first." Peter immediately agreed and taped the second cap to the primer below the first.

"Now for all this junk," said Peter, "It'll all fit down the vent, I think." Peter wound up the unused primer cord while Jimmy collapsed the boxes. They managed to get everything down the hole including the rolled up ladders and the backpacks they had used. Peter had thought it better not to be caught with anything that might arouse suspicion. Let the police gather what evidence they could from whatever is left of this. Peter uncoiled both lengths of fuse toward the back of the roof. Jimmy eased himself over the edge and felt for the dumpster wall. Peter lit a match and set both fuses burning. He was on the ground 20 seconds behind Jimmy.

They took their time as they made their way back toward the park. Jimmy gave John a signal to pick them up. He felt the joint exhilaration of adrenaline and joy and it was unlike anything he had ever experienced. John was alongside before they reached the park.

"Well?" said John.

"Twenty-five, thirty minutes and that place is gone," Peter said confidently. "We need to get some miles between us and it, then get rid of these gloves and we'll be home free." They headed east on the business loop and at the edge of town took the outer road to a creek where Peter dropped the gloves into the running water. Jimmy put the radio in the trunk and got behind the wheel as John took the passenger seat and powered up the notebook for a final wipe on the now useless, but still incriminating computer files.

It was not yet 4:30 a.m. as Peter turned the key in the ignition of his own car at the Kingdom City truck stop. At the same time, one safety fuse won the race to the primer by a full six inches. In an instant, the pace of the fire Peter had set accelerated from a leisurely three seconds per inch to a nimble four miles per second as the explosion carried down the primer cord and into the dynamite and explosives that filled the flue. The brick fireplace instantly shattered, grenade-like, sending masonry through windows, doors, furniture and the entire reception area.

The back room was worse. The explosion removed everything from the procedure room adjacent to the fireplace sending its equipment and walls into the other rearward rooms. Overhead, the stars looked down through a dusty ten foot hole to a spot where no woman would lie down to have her unborn child taken that day.

The first officer on the scene was the same patrolman that had been checking the clinic all night. He was followed by another twenty police, firemen, arson investigators and federal agents. Days later they were still sifting through the wreckage when two young boys rode up on bicycles and advised one investigator that he might like to know that something like a rope ladder was stuck high in a tree about a block down the street. The conspirators had done what they set out to do. Their identity would remain a mystery to authorities. A report of suspicious activity near a St. Louis clinic the same night was no help.

Chapter Four

John woke about 7:30 and soon stood adjusting his tie in the mirror. He hadn't intended to leave so early but there was no food in the apartment, so he left to find breakfast on the way to the Royal Regency. He ate carefully but still managed to get food on his shirt. Nothing a trip to the restroom wouldn't cure. But even with dawdling and cleaning up he still arrived at the hotel ahead of Gary Reed, the Food and Beverage manager at the Regency.

John thought how handy it was that the personnel director was out of town and he would get to see Reed instead of some busybody of a personnel manager. He was amused at how every one of those guys he had ever met acted as if they knew everything when typically they knew next to nothing about the jobs they were paid to fill. John's idea of a personnel manager was one who believed himself to be an expert judge of potential managers but couldn't himself manage a Cub Scout meeting; who hired maids but had never turned a mattress; and evaluated bartender talent, but had never mixed a drink. John stopped himself. He needed to be wide-eyed and uncynical this morning. Got to stay positive and anyway, it was unchristian to be judging some fellow he'd never met.

Reed did not usually get to his office before mid-morning unless an especially important event deserved his attention. The President of the United States had eaten the last breakfast banquet noteworthy enough to merit his personal observation. John hurriedly filled out the employment application only to wait another half-hour before Reed arrived. Whatever John was expecting of the Food and Beverage manager, Gary Reed was not it. Reed was a huge man, well over six feet, red-faced, loud and immediately intimidating. Alarming was the adjective that crossed John's mind as John realized that Reed would have looked more natural with a great, bushy beard, prison tattoos and a Harley Davidson beneath him.

Reed scavenged a cup of coffee and picked up John's application and motioned for John to come into his office. John followed him in and sat in front of the wide desk. John was expecting the worst, but as soon as Reed sat down, the big man assumed a more human, and humane, form. Gary Reed turned out to be warm and good humored. Considering that Reed would not normally even meet entry level food service people, John had to appreciate Reed's seemingly genuine interest in his life, family and interests. Reed spent fifteen minutes before he asked John the first job-related question. The contrast between the initial Reed and the real Reed was such a relief that John wondered if he didn't cultivate it.

"I see you have experience as a bartender. That's good. Is any of this food service experience?" Reed asked.

"Yes, sir," John replied truthfully. Under Jimmy's influence, John had recently been turning into a teetotaler, but he realized those principles might have to be set aside for the moment. "When I worked the bar I had to do every job during the slow times. Sometimes I worked as the evening supervisor. I can mix drinks, wait tables, and I can cook if I need to, but I really like to be out front with the customers."

"You know this is not your local pub. Why do you want to work at the Regency?"

"Well a couple reasons. I've been in school but never got my degree. I intend to go back part-time next fall and eventually to finish up with a degree in Food Service Management. I need a job to get some money put away for school, but I'm also looking for a career in this business. I am here because this is the best hotel in this city. I stayed here once a long time ago with my parents and there was no question this would be my first choice. Actually, I won't even apply anywhere else unless you say you won't hire me."

Reed liked this young man and wanted to hire him on the spot, but had to tell him, "I'm afraid I don't have any openings for a supervisor or even a bartender. Would you be interested in serving and clearing tables and maybe some work in the kitchen?"

"Yes. Yes. When do you want me?"

"Today," said Reed. "Be back here this afternoon at 2:00. We'll get you into a uniform, get your paperwork filled out, and then start your training. I need you to be serving tables tomorrow night."

"I'll be here. Thanks." For a moment John had forgotten why he was taking this job. Reed seemed like a decent man and might well be pleasant to work for. Upon accepting the offer, John had almost said, "Thanks, you won't regret this," but he sobered quickly and reflected that Gary Reed might well regret it six months from now. John was glad for getting in so effortlessly. Still, he thought that if he'd known Reed wouldn't even bother to check his references before hiring him, he might have puffed his credentials a bit more and started a little higher up the ladder. No matter though. He was right where he set out to be. Jimmy had been right about what was available at the hotel. Of course Jimmy knew what happened all over the hotel, since he had been working there for more than a month as a janitor.

John had only two tasks to accomplish during the next three months: learn everything possible about the hotel and work himself into a position of trust that would permit him to move about freely without raising suspicion. The first would come naturally. The second would take some work. That was all right because John was highly motivated, an uncommon trait in any business. John would make it a 12 hour a day job.

It had been four weeks since John began serving tables at the Royal Regency. While he had been originally hired to work thirty hours a week, John caught on fast, and was willing to work anytime. Now he was working fifty and when he finished his shift he would hang around the back room reading manuals. It was 9:00 p.m. and John was reading the monthly maintenance procedures for the Bunn® coffeemaker, when Julie Dermott stopped to see why John was still in the back room. Julie was John's supervisor on the evening shift. She was barely five feet tall, looked ten years younger than her twenty-five years, and worked like a machine. She was both pretty and smart and John knew that if she had not been recently married, he most certainly would be falling in love with her. Considering his real reason for taking the job, John realized that emotional attachments could only make his task more difficult. Even so, he always enjoyed working with her.

"John, are you after my job?" she asked him.

"Sure, Julie," he answered smiling, "but I thought I'd help get you promoted first. You did say I was making you look good, didn't you?"

"What do we do about Tariq?" she joked. Mohammed Tariq was the banquet manager and the one person at the Regency that John truly disliked. John had seen the sharp-nosed, little man terrorize his subordinates over the most petty matters. If things were running smoothly, Tariq would stare icily. If anything were amiss—and in Tariq's view something usually was—he would verbally dismember his erring subordinate in his thickest Persian accent. If he were specially angry, he would lapse into his native tongue so that the only recognizable sound was the word "American," obviously used as a curse of some sort. It was probably a credit to John's work that Moe Tariq had never said anything to suggest he even knew that John existed.

"Things have a way of working out, but if it puts you at ease, I think I'll quit for the night," John told Julie as he rose and put the book back on the shelf. "See you tomorrow." John drove home to his apartment as he always did on the evening shift. The trip from the time clock to his front door took five minutes. John didn't recognize the car in the parking lot until Peter stepped into the light. "I wasn't expecting you so soon, buddy," John said as he grabbed up one of Peter's bags. John hadn't seen Peter for two months and there would be a lot to talk about. They went inside.

John already had the second bedroom furnished for Peter, but Peter made it clear he would not stay long. Peter had no need to be in Kansas City so far in advance of his real business there. Peter knew that John was the key to free access to the hotel and he was apparently getting on well in his new job.

"So do you see Jimmy at all?" Peter asked. "We need to meet, all of us."

"I see him all the time, but we don't really talk since I'm not supposed to know him. We may soon enjoy having distance between Jimmy and us once things get close. I know that security will become a very big issue by the time of the conference. It won't help anything if his record turns up and you and I are associated with him. If we need to meet, we can send him a message tonight."

The next night Jimmy came over to the apartment after he and John were off work. Peter had spent the day familiarizing himself with the city in the area of the hotel. He returned to the apartment with hot pizza and garlic bread. The trio ate as they reviewed their plans and progress.

Peter was pleased to hear how things were going. Jimmy had been working at the Regency for two months as a custodian. He was ideally placed to gather information. Every day, Jimmy emptied dozens of wastebaskets including that of the Director of Hotel Security. He had learned that the Association of Abortion Services Providers was indeed very concerned about security. They would pay for security checks of every hotel employee with access to the main functions at the conference. That meant John and it meant Peter, but would not include Jimmy. There would be metal detectors and armed security at every entrance. The FBI was sending a consultant to review procedures.

"Jimmy, we need to know exactly what precautions they will be taking, so keep your eyes open," Peter reminded. "We should be well placed to deal with anything they do but we must know what we are up against."

John also reported an ideal situation. The banquet staff was the perfect placement for both him and Peter. They would have the run of the entire area around the big ballroom, the only room capable of holding the entire conference.

"Have you thought about where we can put a bomb inside the room?" asked Peter.

"When we have a banquet, there are the guest tables and chairs filling most of the floor. Against the long back wall there is a raised platform holding the head table and podium. Lots of open space under the platform."

"And an obvious place to check for a bomb beforehand," Peter pointed out.

John continued. "For the guests who are still thirsty after the reception there will probably be several drink bars set up around the perimeter of the room. Those bars have a fair amount of space underneath. Room for lots of extra soda tanks and such, but they are mostly left empty from what I can see."

John sketched the room layout for Peter. Jimmy was already familiar with it to some extent. The ballroom was rectangular. Guests entered through two sets of quadruple doors on one long side. There were actually four sets of doors on that side but the two nearer the ends always seemed to be kept locked when the big room was in use. Across from the entrance doors were six doors to the kitchen area. These were also near the center of the longer wall.

"Where would the bars be set up?" Peter asked.

"Between the entrance doors and on each end of the room," John said. "We need to be looking at those, don't we?"

"Unless you have a better idea, that's where we'll start," Peter agreed. "I will be working on getting the materials together to build the bombs. No burning fuses this time. We are going to have to set these things up well in advance. I've got plenty of time to pull my end together. John, you had the tough job and it looks like you already have the run of the place. Can you get me hired?"

"When?"

"Well, we are just over three months away. I need a month to pull my end together. I ought to be working at the hotel a month before the conference. Looks like I need a job by the end of February. Do you think it will be a problem?" John shook his head. "Jimmy, you're our eyes and ears. We have to know what is going on behind the scenes, especially in security. Don't get caught."

Before Jimmy left they arranged to upgrade the access security on Jimmy's computer. Three password levels and heavily encrypted messages would keep any other eyes from the work. Peter left in the morning and did not return for the month he had predicted. Once he logged on to leave a message to John: "Do you use any sort of plastic bags at the hotel that can hold 5-10 gallons of liquid." John answered yes. The hotel had half a dozen items that came in boxes with five-gallon plastic bladders inside.

$$\maltese \quad \maltese \quad \maltese$$

Moe had stopped to speak to John during last night's shift. John was certainly puzzled that the first time Tariq ever said anything to him directly it had been some bland small talk about the Royals' prospects in the upcoming baseball season. John still suspected nothing when Julie sent him to Tariq's office the next afternoon. Julie came in behind him, smiling.

The news was good and John took it as a sign that God had indeed blessed their cause. He was genuinely pleased when Tariq announced that Julie would replace the day supervisor who had left without apparent reason. Julie had not yet been married a year and she would finally be on the same

schedule as her husband. John immediately accepted the offer to take Julie's job on the evening shift. The timing was
perfect. John had been at the Regency for three months and it
was time to get Peter on the staff. Peter had already been in
town for a week and John had intended to bring his name up
to Julie.

"Mr. Tariq, I know a good man to take my job. He's a
great worker, he's new in town and needs the job."

"Send him to personnel. If he looks OK we will hire
him to start tomorrow. You start tomorrow too," Tariq told
him.

"Thank you, sir." John was grinning when he got up to
leave. Julie was smiling too, clearly as pleased at John's pro-
motion as she was at her own move.

It soon became apparent that Peter had assigned each man's
duties with a near perfect assessment of each man's
strengths; and each man's weaknesses. Had Peter been
charged with John's responsibility to rise into a supervisory
position, Peter would have burned six months just trying to
master the one-handed carry of a tray full of entrées. As it
turned out, Peter was no waiter and would have to bear down
just to avoid being noticed and dismissed by Moe Tariq.

Peter, unlike John, only worked twenty hours a week.
Still he felt pressed for time for he had yet to finalize the form
of the bomb and then put it together and get it into place at
the hotel. As the time neared, Peter and John had no direct
contact with Jimmy, except by way of encrypted computer
messages, most of which were from Jimmy to them.

Jimmy learned well in advance that he too was about
to come under the microscope of security precautions. "Isn't
this handy," Jimmy thought as he made his nightly stop in
the security director's office, "and it beats sifting trash." Apparently, the abortionist's convention was looming so large on
the security manager's agenda that he had created an ex-
haustive checklist setting out tasks and deadlines dealing ex-

clusively with security at that convention. Jimmy had long appreciated the sloppiness of this security manager; sloppiness even as he got organized. How convenient that he was too lazy even to turn off the copy machine when he left in the evening. Jimmy quickly copied the security checklist and collected his trash quota before leaving and locking the office.

Through Jimmy's work the conspirators were able to anticipate every roadblock they might encounter. They learned that everything would have to be in place 24 hours before convention registration began. After that, outside security would be in place. There would be checks of incoming packages. There would be machines designed to detect explosives. It would soon become clear to Peter that simply planting one or more devices inside a portable bar or under the dais would be asking for discovery. Whatever bomb sniffers or dogs did not uncover, a careful search would. It was also clear that Jimmy's career as an anti-abortion activist would soon be discovered and he would then be eliminated as a source of information. Indeed, the ASP punch list included criminal record checks for every hotel employee.

Jimmy scanned the pages of the security punchlist into his computer and the graphics file was waiting for John at his next download. John brought the image up on his screen the next morning and began to read. Then he stopped. "Why do you suppose hotel security would be in contact with Mason Wolfe's senior assistant?" he asked Peter. Mason Wolfe, former congressman from Kentucky, had been confirmed quickly as President Kerner's replacement for Secretary of State Vincent, who had died a suicide just weeks before. Already Wolfe had mediated a settlement in a centuries-old ethnic conflict that had defied all prior attempts at resolution. Despite Wolfe's disclaimer of any credit in the matter and his apparent humility at this initial success, the world press was clamoring for more of Mason Wolfe.

Who was the essentially unknown former congressman from Kentucky? That was the question posed and the question that every newsmagazine and television network was scrambling to answer. "You grew up in Kentucky, John," said Peter. "You ought to be the expert on Mason Wolfe."

"I sure am," he said as he remembered old feelings of betrayal by the traitor Wolfe, "I remember when he was just obscure slime. Now he's famous slime. What else would you like to know about him?"

"Let's get another message up to Jimmy tonight. Since he will soon be discovered as a suspicious character, we can't afford to use computer messaging further," Peter said as John brought his editor up on the computer screen, "Remind him to do a security file wipe and a complete hard drive optimization. When this is over, it's Jimmy who is going to have half a dozen government agencies inside his house. To tell the truth, I'd feel better if he dropped that computer in the river, but this should do the trick."

"I'll do the same with my machine," John replied.

"Drop it in the river?"

"No way. I'll just clean off the drive. Meanwhile, we have our drop at the hotel if something urgent comes up," he continued, referring to emergency plans they had made to exchange messages inside the hotel.

Two days later John and Peter learned along with everyone else at work that Wolfe was to speak at the convention. ASP had only recently asked Congressman Wolfe to be their guest as the year's ASP "Friend of Choice." Organizers understandably radiated their delight when they were able to announce that the new and now acclaimed Secretary of State would address the convention. Wolfe not only agreed to honor his original commitment but would also give the keynote address on the second night of the convention.

Peter was now running all out as the convention approached. Each night, at the end of the evening shift, John would deliberately take his time in finishing up his paperwork. Once the others had left, Peter would carefully explore the building with an eye to hidden areas; areas that would hold his packages while withstanding all security efforts to defeat him.

Within a week, Peter had crystallized a plan to fit the building, the schedule, and the conspirators' objective: to kill as many abortionists as possible at one blow. Together, Peter and John agreed that only one place was suitable for placing the explosives: above the false ceiling in the main ballroom. Twenty-five feet high, the ceiling was reached by ladders going up the wall of the adjacent kitchen. The crawl space contained low catwalks normally used for reaching lights, air ducts and other utilities.

"We can do this with three devices," Peter said. "Two would be well away from the ladders and across the room over each entrance. The last would be directly between the ladders over the head table and speaker's platform below."

"Is there a way to set them off all at the same time?" John asked.

"A lighted fuse obviously won't work," Peter explained. Instead they would use a radio controller of the type used to fly a model airplane. The control box had just two radio switches. The first switch would start the charging of a capacitor on each detonator, the same way a camera flash must first charge for a few seconds before it could fire. The second switch would send the high voltage charge to the electric blasting cap, thereby setting off the explosive. "There will be plenty of bang in these things, each one more powerful than the one we used in Columbia," said Peter, "but that won't be enough to get the job done. The explosive we use will produce fire as well as blast and we can build on that. How many of those liquid shortening containers have we collected?"

"Well, we have ten here and there are a few more tucked away at work," John answered.

"Each one of those will contain five gallons of jellied gasoline. It's easy to make, just plastic foam mixed with gas."

"So that's what all that stuff in your room is for."

Peter continued, "So with each bomb surrounded with twenty gallons of napalm, there is no way anyone will get out of that room alive."

"My God, Peter, I guess I hadn't thought exactly how it would happen," John said as he stared off into the corner.

Then he asked, "We can do this after the dinner is cleared and our people are out of the room?"

"Our people?" Peter asked as he looked at John. He paused and then nodded saying, "Yes, after dinner." John could see Peter was annoyed at the suggestion of complications that did not really concern him.

During the week before the convention, Jimmy checked his work schedule and realized that the results of the criminal records check had come back. Jimmy was scheduled to work daily through the next Tuesday and then off until Saturday. Not coincidentally, the convention would run from Wednesday afternoon until Friday noon. Jimmy had half-expected to be fired rather than rescheduled, but he had, after all, been honest when he noted on his application his conviction for violating an injunction. Until two days before, the hotel management hardly knew what an injunction was, let alone care how Jimmy had violated one. All the same, Jimmy knew that after Tuesday, he would not work at the Royal Regency again. He also knew that the convention would be over at 8:30 p.m. Thursday, not noon Friday.

The week before the convention passed quickly. Peter was constantly busy, both at the hotel and at the apartment, while John kept to his duties as evening supervisor. John arranged for Peter's access and opportunity to transport and assemble the bombs unseen, so that by Tuesday midnight all was in place. Peter had been given short schedules and back room assignments while everyone else was concerned with serving meals. Doors were left unlocked. Several trips to and from the apartment on each of three nights were sufficient.

Although the ceiling space was supposed to provide quick access to utilities it was hardly designed for easy hauling of fifty pound boxes and the other gear that Peter had bought or constructed over the preceding months. The lighting was strictly minimal to begin with and Peter had already gone to the trouble to replace the light bulbs in the widely spaced sockets with others of more modest output. When he had finished, none of his devices would be apparent to one who might climb either ladder and switch on the lights for an inspection.

On Tuesday night, Peter finished the three bombs, each with its radio-controlled detonator and powerful explosive, all surrounded by Peter's homemade napalm. Peter was concerned that the radio batteries might not last until Thursday night, so he planned to go back up to activate each receiver on Wednesday night. Security would have tightened by that time but Peter and John were both scheduled Wednesday and Thursday and were confident that Peter could get up the ladder unseen for the five minutes it would take to activate the three switches.

On Wednesday, John came in early to see what security measures were being taken. As John arrived, Moe Tariq quickly caught him and introduced him to Agent Stone, a grim faced man in a gray suit. John had never imagined that he would be discussing convention security with the Secret Service, but he was soon telling Stone everything he knew about each employee that he supervised. The ascension of Mason Wolfe to the President's cabinet had hiked the level of risk and it seemed that security precautions had increased proportionately. Tariq offered John's services as the agent's tour guide and together they began to explore the area of the kitchen and ballroom. Every door, storeroom and refrigerator was investigated.

Agent Stone reached up and laid his hand on a rung and asked, "What's up this ladder?"

"That's the utility access to the space above the ceiling," John answered. John thought the man must certainly hear his heart racing. Stone began to climb.

"Locked?"

"I don't know," John said as he watched as the agent's head disappeared into the hole in the kitchen ceiling

"Is there a light up here?"

"There's supposed to be a switch, but I've never actually been up there," he lied. Stone found the switch and John watched him climb inside and disappear. Stone was gone a minute. Then two. No sound. John wondered if he had found them yet. Finally, the government man emerged and came down the ladder.

"Got a sink to wash my hands?" he asked.

"Right over here." John stepped on the faucet pedal and the Secret Service man rinsed off.

"Is there any other way up there?" he asked.

John led him to the other end of the prep area and showed him an identical ladder rising to the ceiling space. The agent seemed satisfied and did not investigate further.

"Unless I am here to check any delivery, these outside doors stay locked until the banquet is over tomorrow night. I'll be around until then. Just call your security office if you need to use the doors and we'll manage it." When they finished with the back room, they started out toward the main room, which was being cleaned up after the noon meal. "Do you know a fellow who works here named Jimmy Anderson?"

"He doesn't work in this area, does he?" said John.

"He's in housekeeping. I just wondered if you knew him," Stone said as if it was not worth discussing further. John explained how the banquet room would be set up for the ASP dinner Thursday and the agent seemed interested in it all. Clearly, it would have been impossible to place a bomb on the main floor while the Secret Service was around. No way to get it in the building; no way to get it into a portable bar or under the dais until it was too late. Even then, places so easy to check certainly would be.

John sat down to work on the next week's schedule until the time he was scheduled to start work. He realized the schedule would never be posted, but he needed something to divert his attention from the coming day's events. Except for providing cover for Peter, John had nothing whatever to do with the plan at this point; just stay on the job until 8:15 Thursday evening, then take his regular break.

Peter arrived later and learned about Agent Stone's visit up the ladder. Now that the kitchen exits had been locked and the area searched, security was more or less a matter of controlling who and what came in. Peter had no problem getting into the ceiling later to activate the radio-controlled detonators. Three high explosive bombs, each enhanced to spread fire with its blast, awaited the signal from Peter's controller.

John arrived home soon after Peter. He sat down next to Peter at the kitchen table. "Have you considered," he said, "that tomorrow we are going to send hundreds of abortionists to hell?"

"No, we aren't," Peter disagreed with his usual shortness. He thought a second and added: "They bought their ticket a long time ago. The train leaves tomorrow. As Jimmy explains it, the timing is a great favor to these people. If you shoot one of these serial killers at work he's either about to commit a dozen murders or just finished washing the blood of a dozen off his hands. This way he's had two, maybe three days in a row where he hasn't killed a single person—a rarity for these criminals."

"It doesn't matter anyway. We are in a revolution. This is a war and we are doing what we've been called to do. Look, we've spent years trying to get to the abortionists' conscience, to save the children and even to save the killer's soul. But that's done. This time tomorrow the state of his soul will be an individual matter between him and his Judge." It was the most Peter had ever said about what he thought he was doing. John had worked this all out in his mind before he agreed to do it, but he still could not avoid wincing at the reality that lay ahead.

John lay in bed and thought about Thursday night. He was glad that Wolfe would be there. The man was a deceitful, evil hypocrite and yet he became more celebrated with each new year. In just 24 hours they could all mourn him.

How many unborn children will live because three hundred abortionists do not return to work on Monday morning? Some of these guys do 5000 a year. John had figured close to a million more babies would survive the coming year. It would be impossible for the remaining butchers to pick up all the slack, John thought. All the real activists are here, along with their clinic administrators. Who knows how many of the stay-at-homes will lose their nerve and quit the dirty business. When John rose the next day, he doubted whether he had slept even one hour.

"You'll send me on break at 8:00 tonight, right?" Peter confirmed.

"Right. And I'll take a break at 8:15," said John, "Since you will go outside to set it off, I wonder if I would arouse less suspicion if I stayed inside. Shouldn't it be safe in the lounge? It's practically in a separate building."

"Well, you better be sitting in the restroom when it goes, because there could be glass flying everywhere."

John had been on duty about thirty minutes when he noticed Julie getting ready to leave for the day. "I'm so glad to hear your news," John heard one of the waiters say to her.

"What news?" John asked as Julie turned to leave.

"I'm pregnant! Sorry, I can't talk. I'm in a hurry," she said with a smile, then walked out the door to the main hall.

John managed a quick, "Good for you," before she was gone. "And good for you Julie *that you are gone,*" he added to himself.

⊕   ⊕   ⊕

Dinner was finished and the tables had been cleared when Peter walked up to John and said to him: "I'm going on break." John nodded and Peter walked out of the banquet hall toward the main lobby. ASP's President was making introductions at the microphone. At the last minute, television cameras had been let into the hall. Two were already sending pictures to a truck waiting in the parking lot.

Ten minutes later Mason Wolfe rose to deafening applause, which Wolfe withstood with seeming embarrassment. He thanked the leadership and launched into praise of the daily work of the membership. "This association has done more than any other group to better the lives of the poor. All the public housing; all the food stamps; all the early education programs, all of these well-meaning, but misguided efforts, are nothing compared to the good that comes to all society when a child is born to a woman who is prepared to care for it; born to a family who will raise that child to be a productive, intelligent citizen."

It was dark outside as Peter reached his car and removed the controller from the trunk. He set it on the seat of the car and started the engine.

"You are the vanguard of this movement," Wolfe told his audience, "You provide options beyond a welfare check. You bring hope to a pregnant young woman who despairs even for life itself." Wolfe spoke calmly and without interruption by applause. If there had been but one camera in the room it would have given the impression that Wolfe was speaking in a graveyard, so quiet was his audience; but the real scene was on the faces of the guests. Each watched and listened intently as Wolfe gave voice to what they knew in their hearts: No slogans about individual choices and women's bodies; this was a man with compassion for the whole of Humanity; a man with enthusiasm for its future. They had known him as a friend, but they had not really known him. Now he spoke words they knew were true even if they had not thought those things before. He spoke of the tragedy of poor families burdened with children they cannot feed, let alone educate. "It is a crime for children to be born to such poverty, such ignorance. We are in a war for survival and the danger is so great that we can no longer stand by as our planet's limited resources are squandered on the hopelessly wounded."

John checked his watch. "Two minutes and I'm gone," he thought. He had been pushing the thought of this hour from his mind all day, but now the bombs overhead filled his consciousness.

"Still, there are those who cling to a medieval worldview," Wolfe continued. "They must be won over. There are stubborn and powerful organizations, such as the Church of Rome, whose male hierarchy continues to foster our collective suicide."

Peter stopped the car one block away from the Regency. He had tested the transmitter and knew it was good for three times that distance. This would do fine. He flipped the first of two switches. Above the heads of eight hundred entranced guests, three capacitors began to sing softly as each detonator charged itself. Julie Dermott had left work early that day to make a first visit to her doctor. Now she stopped back at the hotel to collect some paperwork she had left undone.

John looked at his watch: 8:15 p.m. He reached the main doors and met Julie coming in. John made a decision even before he spoke. He would betray himself and probably Peter but he would not leave her in this building.

"Julie, you can't stay," John started to explain.

"We can no longer afford to indulge those who believe in religious myths; myths that blind us all to our evolutionary duties to ourselves, to our planet and to our children," Mason Wolfe, warned. "No God will save us; we must save ourselves."

"Why, what's wrong?" Julie asked. John took her by the arm as he stepped through the doorway.

Peter looked toward the hotel as he pushed the second switch. Inside, a curtain of fire descended from above. The camera between the entrances was about ten feet from where John had intercepted Julie and was aimed close in on the speaker. It registered a flash and then nothing else. The other camera, which was making a longer shot from one end of the room had survived a split second longer.

Chapter Five

And then that wicked one shall be revealed . . . whose coming is according to the working of Satan, in all power, and signs, and lying wonders.

—II Thessalonians 2: 8-9

Peter entered the anteroom of a suite in another hotel miles from the Regency. The burly man that met him at the door told him to take a seat and wait. The television was monopolized by special reports on every network showing half the Royal Regency in flames. The injured were everywhere in the background as a reporter offered a still sketchy outline: "Eyewitnesses say that less than an hour ago this tremendous fire began with an explosion that shook this area of downtown Kansas City, Missouri. Many people have been injured and we have reports of some fatalities."

The picture switched suddenly back to the network anchor as she introduced a videotape, which had just been released by a Kansas City television station. "We have just received a report that the Association of Abortion Service Providers was meeting at the Royal Regency Hotel in Kansas City this evening. These pictures have just come in." Peter watched as ASP President Schmeer introduced various dignitaries including some last minute additions eager to be seen at the table with the new Secretary of State. Two congressmen, one each from Kansas and Missouri, had come. The Governor and the state Attorney General managed to be in town. Any one of them might have held the podium alone that night, but this night they came because Wolfe had come. Peter had not realized that so many VIP's had turned out. There were camera pans of the assembled dinner guests.

The screen returned to Mason Wolfe. He was gesturing, his arm over his head. Was very nearly raging, as he repeated: ". . . .We must save ourselves." Wolfe brought the arm down as if hurling a thunderbolt just as a flash consumed him from above. The picture went from intense white to chaotic static in an instant.

The familiar anchor's face returned, but for seconds she said nothing, then with an obvious tear on her cheek she spoke, "A hotel spokesperson has reported that 800 guests were scheduled to attend the ASP banquet this evening. No word at this hour on the fate of those inside at the time of the explosion."

"And no need to wonder after those pictures," Peter muttered. He watched for another fifteen minutes as more pictures and reports came in from outside the hotel. It soon became clear that none of the victims or eyewitnesses shown so far had been inside the main ballroom when the bombs had gone off.

"Not one. Not one of them got out," Peter thought as he shook his head from side to side and smiled. He had done his job well and he was here to get his money. He couldn't be sure of John's fate, but Peter knew it was but a matter of time before the investigation turned upon the new banquet supervisor at the Royal. They would find John's computer with the trail of incriminating messages Peter had left on it after John left for work. Jimmy, at least, would be in custody within a day of its discovery.

If the world hadn't already figured out who had toasted 300 abortionists, along with 500 hundred of their closest friends, it soon would. Once the news outlets got a look at Jimmy the fanatic Christian, everyone would know who had killed the Governor, two Congressmen and the Secretary of State. The same messages would falsely implicate several prominent Catholic leaders who had failed to follow the leadership of the American bishops in declaring a moratorium on outspoken opposition to the abortion trade.

Naturally, Peter's planted messages had been sanitized and his own name would not appear on John's machine. Peter took the extra step of deleting the files after he loaded them. That would serve the dual purpose of keeping John—if he had somehow got back to the machine—from seeing the altered files; and also giving the appearance that some attempt had been made to remove the incriminating files. Never mind that such files would become immediately readable by anyone who was actually looking for them.

Peter's reverie was broken by the man who had let him in. "He will speak to you now, Mr. Hancock," said the man, motioning Peter to follow. He did not notice the bulk of the nine-millimeter handgun under the doorman's jacket. The next room was just a bit darker than the front room and Peter huddled his shoulders at a sudden chill that met him as he entered. A taller man stood looking out a picture window. Several miles away, toward downtown, the flashing lights of a hundred emergency vehicles were visible in the distance beyond the tall man.

Peter wondered if this were the shadowy individual who led the Society that employed him. Perhaps he would now learn whom it was that needed 800 people dead and at the same time wanted it blamed on the Christians. He sensed that the events of this night were far larger than he had suspected. He felt power in this man and pride deceived Peter into believing he had a part in that power.

"Are you the one?" Peter found himself saying.

"I am he," said the man, turning into the light. The words came like a blow and Peter fell back and very nearly down. Then he saw the noble, but now cruel, face. "Is it hard to look upon he whom you have killed? I am alive and risen from among the dead!" proclaimed Mason Wolfe.

Peter dropped to his knees and cried, "My Lord," then lowered his head to the floor. Wolfe turned and walked away. Peter did not see him motion to the doorman. He did not hear the gun go off behind his head.

Auxiliary Bishop Brendan Shea of St. Louis was in the city for meetings of the Kansas and Missouri bishops when he first heard reports of the bombing. Within fifteen minutes he was in a cab on his way to the Missouri side. The emergency room at Downtown Hospital near the Royal Regency was filled with the injured. Many were dying.

The scene Brendan Shea discovered was being repeated at hospitals all around the city that night. He appeared as an ordinary priest, without any trappings of his office. Some of the staff would occasionally direct him to one or another patient. Otherwise he attracted little attention in the chaos as he moved through the hallways administering comfort and anointing.

Brendan had finished giving the last sacrament to a young woman, no more than nineteen or twenty years old, who had been found outside the banquet hall in the lobby area of the hotel. Burned and bloody, she had died shortly after arriving just a few minutes before.

There was a sudden commotion of lights and people at the emergency room entrance and Brendan saw a television reporter with a camera in tow. The reporter appeared to be looking for someone or something in particular but was obviously disappointed. After a brief exchange the television crew obeyed the staff's orders and went back outside where they would be out of the way. Brendan did not at first understand what interest they would have in coming into this place when the main story and even more wounded bodies could be seen at the hotel.

The question soon was answered, for moments later a lone man strode into the entrance of the emergency room. Every eye that was not immediately occupied fell on the man.

Brendan saw a tall kingly figure he thought he recognized, but in this place, it did not immediately register that the man was Mason Wolfe. No one expects the United States' Secretary of State to appear in a Kansas City emergency room, so it took Brendan a few moments to place the familiar face.

"Wolfe," he finally said to himself remembering that the Secretary was at the Royal Regency that night. He noted that Wolfe must not have been inside the hotel when the bomb exploded. Wolfe was absolutely uninjured; clean and well dressed. With his proud angular face and nose like Chief Sitting Bull, Wolfe had a look of complete confidence. Brendan thought he had never seen a human being display such lofty arrogance and he wondered what business Wolfe could possibly have in such a place. Like most of the staff, Brendan had not watched the newscasts long enough to see the tape of Wolfe's speech. If he had, he would have been even more perplexed at Wolfe's appearance at the entrance.

Wolfe looked once in each direction and then turned deliberately to his left and marched down the wing from which Brendan was watching. As Wolfe started down the hallway, the camera crew hurried in and followed him down the hall. Wolfe walked straight toward Brendan who could not help feeling that Wolfe was here for him, or because of him. He quickly prayed, "What do I do, Lord?"

"Step away from the girl," came a voice inside his head but clear as if spoken in his ear. Brendan had never received such an answer before, but he obeyed instantly and stepped across the hallway and away from the girl's body.

Mason Wolfe stopped where the girl lay. The camera closed in as Wolfe looked upon the girl's covered body. His eyes moistened as he gently pulled back the sheet to reveal the abused head. The camera crew had left the superfluous reporter behind and just let the videotape unwind. Clearly, Mason Wolfe was not here to answer questions. Everyone in the area had stopped what they were doing and watched to see what came next; everyone except one doctor who had not seen Wolfe walk in and now followed him down the hall. The doctor was about to confront the intruder when Wolfe right-faced toward the doctor and demanded in a loud voice: "What is wrong with this woman?"

The doctor shrank back and then answered, "She is dead."

Wolfe turned back and looked at the young woman. He bent low over the still body, closed his eyes and spoke softly. Nearby, Brendan and the doctor, but not the microphones, heard him say: "Thank you, Father and Lord of this World, that you have heard me." Wolfe took the girl's hand, and standing straight again, spoke in a clear voice: "Wake up." Brendan saw her chest move and then her lips. Then he noticed the arm that he had seen so horribly burned was now pink and healthy. The girl opened her eyes and looked at Mason Wolfe. He motioned to the doctor, "Get her some clothes, doctor. She will be fine."

He then faced toward the camera and slowly turned and looked into each face in the now crowded hallway. Finally, his eye fell on the face of Brendan Shea and there it stopped. This time, with back to the camera, no record was made as Wolfe's mouth twisted with rage. The lens only caught the unmoving face of a then unidentified priest standing just beyond Mason Wolfe. Wolfe cast his eyes toward the floor and recomposed himself. It had seemed as if he would now have some words of explanation, but instead he hustled out between the dazed doctor and the camera and was through the double doors before most could comprehend what they had just seen.

Chapter Six

Clement XV, Supreme Pontiff, to the Bishops, Priests and Deacons, Men and Women Religious, and Lay Faithful of the Church of Jesus Christ, Greetings:

For almost a thousand years, the Bishop of Rome has been elected by the College of Cardinals. Throughout the history of the Church, however, the Successor of Peter has had authority to alter the manner by which his successor is chosen.

I choose now to do what has not been done in a thousand years because the problems facing Christ's Church have no precedent, not in a thousand years; nay, not since her founding. My predecessors have spoken of the coming day, the coming final conflict between the Church and the anti-Church. The trials they foresaw in outline, we now see in our midst.

Many of the shepherds have become wolves among the sheep. And the sheep suffer in the trial and rightly wonder why Christ does not answer their prayers and cleanse the temple of His Church. They ask why His Vicar does not remove the wolf and the thief from the sheep pen. They receive no answer, but only exhortation to remain true to OUR LORD and pray. Meanwhile, the wolf is emboldened to plunder still more. I have suffered with you. I have even attempted to remove the wolf from the pen, but the Spirit would not permit it.

As your servant and Christ's, I can only plead that you will continue to bear your suffering in prayer, penance and obedience. I have been given no knowledge of what trials you shall endure when I am gone. I am an old man and will soon lay down this burden. I therefore solemnly declare that upon my death the following Cardinals, or as many of their number as may gather within thirty days, shall convene to elect my successor:

John Cardinal Stewart	England
Timothy Cardinal Reagan	Ireland
Isaac Cardinal Morumba	Zaïre
Suresh Cardinal Koomswami	India
Guiseppi Cardinal Chiavetta	Italy
Francis Cardinal Lombardo	Italy
Gregorio Cardinal Reyes	Philippines
Michael Cardinal Lindsay	United States

The election shall be by a two-thirds majority of those voting and under such other rules as two thirds may adopt. The above-named Cardinals shall convene upon my death in Vatican City or in such other place of their choosing.

Given in Rome, at Saint Peter's, on 16 May, the Feast of Saint Brendan the Navigator, in the eighth year of my Pontificate.

Clement XV

When Cardinal Lindsay finished reading aloud he handed the document to Shea. "Here we have been prodding old Papa Clement to play Pius X with the heretics and give them the boot; and what does he do? He leaves that job to the next man, while at the same time insuring that his election will be accompanied by an uproar. Have you checked to see if this has happened before?"

"Yes, I have," said the younger man, taking some notes from his pocket. "In 530 A.D. Pope Felix III was seriously ill and also faced immediate problems within the Church. Rather than permit the traditional election, he designated Boniface II his successor. The priests of Rome elected another man, Dioscorus, while the few loyal to Felix consecrated Boniface that same day. Boniface II was the true Pope. Dioscorus was an antipope. Boniface himself chose a candidate for his own successor, but later called a synod in which the old electoral system was reinstated. Much later, in 1059, Pope Nicholas II, with the assent of a synod of 113 bishops, designated the College of Cardinals as the body that would select every new pope for the next thousand years."

"Is there any question that Clement has the power to change the rules regarding the selection of his successor?"

"None," replied Brendan Shea.

"Well, Clement may have a few years left in him, so we may not have to deal with this issue for a good while. Changing the subject, Brendan, how are you coming on the report on Mason Wolfe that the Holy Father has asked us to prepare?"

After the Royal Regency bombing, the name Mason Wolfe rapidly became the most famous on earth. His survival from the bombing unscathed, while every other person in that room had died, was so sensational as to be considered miraculous. If skeptics thought his escape merely good fortune, they were at a complete loss to explain the raising of the young woman whom doctors had formally declared dead. Afterward, the doctors noted that a number of other remarkable recoveries had occurred that night in the same emergency room where Wolfe had stunned the world.

Within days, Wolfe turned up in the Middle East announcing another peace between the Arabs and Israel. The difference this time was that the agreement was concluded without the usual bombings and murders by radical groups still disenchanted with the terms of peace. Mason Wolfe had brought all the parties together as no man had before. His acclaim was now universal. Editorials in every language called for his immediate installation as Secretary General of the United Nations. The current holder of that office tendered his resignation contingent upon receiving assurances that Wolfe would accept election. Mason Wolfe ignored the applause and dropped out of sight for a time. Since Wolfe was an American, Pope Clement had personally requested that Cardinal Lindsay submit a confidential report on the wonder working Secretary of State and Brendan Shea had been given the task of drafting that report.

"I have thought a great deal about that night at the hospital in Kansas City," Brendan told Cardinal Lindsay. "That girl had been declared dead only minutes before I gave her the last sacrament. Two minutes later Wolfe is telling her to wake up. I cannot believe that he raised her from the dead, as only God can do that. But I know from the doctors and from my own eyes that she was beyond all earthly help and that Wolfe healed her in a matter of seconds. Perhaps she was not beyond reviving, if somehow she could be healed. And somehow, she was!"

"Now you had just anointed the woman?" the Cardinal asked as he turned away to retrieve his own copy of the Bible.

"Yes, Eminence."

"You have then thought about your own conduct in this case?"

"How do you mean?"

The Cardinal flipped to James chapter five and read the familiar verse: "Is any man sick among you? Let him bring in the priests of the church, and let them pray over him, anointing him with oil in the name of the Lord. And the prayer of faith shall save the sick person."

"But that is impossible!" Brendan protested as he rose to his feet. The Cardinal's notion came as a shock for Brendan.

"Impossible? Bishop Shea, it is not impossible."

"I mean that Wolfe, despite his recent posturing as peacemaker, is no friend of Christ or his Church, and I do not see how God would assist this man by healing the woman through me and letting Wolfe take the credit."

"Well, I understand what you are saying, but I am trying to keep separate what our God does directly and that which He merely permits. There is nothing remarkable about bad men taking credit for the good done by others. God would have to shut down grace altogether to keep that from happening, don't you think, Brendan?"

Once the Cardinal had reframed the issue, Brendan could not deny the obvious possibility. Even so, he needed some time to consider it. "Well let me digest that a bit and just go on to some other things. I believe I've mentioned before that Wolfe seemed to recognize me at the hospital. Not that he knows who I am—we've never been introduced—but he was quite angry when he finally noticed me. And not just my collar, but me. What I have not mentioned before is that a very similar incident occurred between him and me during a chance meeting several years ago." Brendan Shea explained the night at the pro-choice banquet and then launched into a review of the public career of Mason Wolfe.

"Even before the night of the bombing, Wolfe had been making increasingly hostile speeches with regard to Christians in general but reserving his most acid remarks for the

Catholic Church. Whether the issue is human rights, marriage, abortion, euthanasia or population control, Wolfe has staked out positions attacking the Church. I do not need to tell you that after the Pope, you are his favorite target, Eminence."

"I hadn't noticed," the Cardinal said dryly, with a slight smile.

"The legislation he sponsored before he left Congress was stalled at the time, but now after the bombing, Wolfe's measures will become law. Only approved churches will retain a tax-exempt status and we will not qualify. I have sometimes thought the tax deduction was a doubtful benefit to the extent that it sometimes muzzled the Church from speaking out on moral issues. The new law, however, removes the tax-exemption while at the same time making it a crime to publicly condemn most of the new policies. I can remember when you'd have to go to China to be treated like this."

"Then persecution is coming," the Cardinal observed matter of factly. "Do we have any idea of what Wolfe sees as his role in all of this?"

"Well this gets a little interesting. Wolfe is American and as far as anyone can tell so are his parents and grandparents, but relatives say his mother's family came from France in Revolutionary times. Wolfe claims to be descended from the Merovingian kings of Europe. Some say he has a claim to the French monarchy; even to a European monarchy if such a thing were to exist."

"One odd story has him wrapped up in the Grail legend. There are writers who claim that his family possesses the Holy Grail itself. An interviewer once asked Wolfe about the volumes written about his family's possession of secrets underlying the Grail legends and he did not deny it. "

Wolfe is quoted as saying, "The Holy Grail is misrepresented in most of the stories. It is not the Chalice of Christ's Last Supper, nor the vessel that caught His blood as it flowed from the cross. Not some sacred stone brought from the heavens. These things will be better understood later, but I will say that the stories are true that the Grail is a vessel that holds the blood of Jesus."

"Do you know what that might mean?" asked the Cardinal.

"Wolfe has never said anything more to clarify the Grail mystery. But where he lets off, a hundred writers pick up the story. It's a story that has been around for years, but only recently has it been applied to Wolfe. Esoteric and Gnostic groups carried the ball for a while, but now even the tabloids are running the story that Wolfe is not the possessor of the Holy Grail. He is the Holy Grail!"

"The legends conflict, but the story is told that Mary Magdalene, after the crucifixion, brought the Grail to southern Gaul. The supposed secret is the belief that Jesus of Nazareth was married to Mary Magdalene who bore him one or more children before his death. His descendants, so they believed, perpetuated the bloodline in the Jewish community in the south of what is now France for four hundred years. They intermarried with the Franks before the founding of the Merovingian dynasty in the fifth century. So the bloodline of Christ, and of King David, reigned as European kings."

"And so might rule again, I presume."

"That's the story of the secret of the Grail Keepers and why the secret was supposedly of far greater significance than a relic, even a relic of Jesus Christ. And the irony is that the secret—or rather the legend of the Grail—was like a parable with its obvious meaning to the uninitiated and a deeper meaning, known only to a select few. In their belief, the Grail is indeed the vessel of Christ's blood because Christ's blood flows in his veins. From Wolfe's remarks, it is clear that he believes it, or wants others to believe anyway. And the better part of the world is ready to believe anything Mason Wolfe says at this point."

Chapter Seven

Mason Wolfe's prestige seemed to climb with each public appearance. One brilliant public relations event was his appearance with an unknown, but well-spoken young woman named Julie Dermott. She stood at a microphone a few feet from the Secretary of State and paid him tribute. Her face was beautiful, guileless and innocent as a baby's. And her once charred skin showed no signs of the hideous explosion and fire that briefly took her life. She told her story of that night and how Mason Wolfe had given back her life.

"Mr. Wolfe not only saved me," she said turning slightly aside and laying a hand on her obviously growing middle, "but also saved my twin babies." Julie reached toward the Secretary of State and started to cry. "Thank you, Mr. . . ." She could not finish—for the tears rushed out—as she returned Wolfe's embrace. Mason Wolfe cried. The audience cried too; for love of the girl and for the hero that saved her.

If there were only a few men who resisted Mason Wolfe's charms, there were even fewer who were not won by this child-like woman whose inner loveliness transcended her soft dark beauty in a way that the usually cynical news media could only describe as angelic. It was only natural then, that the unemployed former banquet supervisor would pass the remaining months of her pregnancy in constant demand as television guest. A month after the birth of Julie's twin daughters, she hired an agent and was soon scheduled as guest host on a late night talk show. When the ratings numbers were published, it became inevitable that the young mother would have her own show. That the *Julie!* show was a winner came as no surprise to anyone except Julie herself, who gladly accepted, but never understood, her success.

Secretary of State Mason Wolfe never formally declined the invitation to head the United Nations. He simply dismissed all questions on the subject with a wave of the hand or a reference to his work in the service of his country. Many could not understand Wolfe's refusal to serve, but most observers noted that the U.S. Secretary of State could still wield more influence than the leader of a perennially toothless U.N.

The economic power of the United States had been waning for many years. Manufacturing and jobs continued to stream outside the nation's borders. The best that the newest American industries could offer was to replace the lost jobs with jobs paying half of the old wages. The economic strains continued to wear on families, as parents spent more time earning a living and less time civilizing their children. The real growth industries were the illegal drug trade, law enforcement, prison construction and raising taxes to support the ever-increasing demands of the welfare state. Never before had the number of non-working Americans been so large.

Murders, assaults and robberies continued, but increasingly, civil disorder and terrorism were the subject of the evening news. As government became more oppressive in its indiscriminate crackdown, the vicious circle escalated with even more threats and reprisals against government agents and buildings. The moral climate paralleled the economic and crime problems. Psychiatrists and other mental health professionals struggled mightily to keep their reference manuals updated with new and previously unthinkable perversions.

Month after month, events had combined to weaken the world-wide influence of the United States as Americans saw their economy eclipsed by the economic power of the oriental nations, especially China, and the newly formed and vigorous United States of Europe. The shift in the global balance of power clearly demonstrated that Mason Wolfe's growing influence had less to do with his office and everything to do with Wolfe himself.

The seismic activity that had recently caused so much devastation in both North and South America began to be mirrored around the globe. New volcanoes appeared and those once dead sprang to life pouring sulfur dioxide and ash into the skies.

Weather was strongly affected and became marked by extremes: droughts in the grain belts and floods in the deserts. Food shortages were pushing prices upward everywhere. Where the want of food grew into famine, disease quickly followed. One very localized earthquake, however, would have a greater consequence than any of the other many and increasing disturbances in the earth.

The ancient city of Jerusalem is a focal point for Judaism, Islam and Christianity. Three thousand years ago the city became Israel's capital when it was conquered by King David. Solomon's great temple on Mount Moriah in Jerusalem became the center of Jewish worship. There, the Holy Ark of the Covenant was kept; and there the priests carried out the animal sacrifice as required by the Torah. King Nebuchaddnezer in 587 B.C destroyed the Temple in the Babylonian conquest. In time, the Jews were permitted to return from their Babylonian captivity and Zerubbabel rebuilt the Jewish temple on a more modest scale.

After the conquests of Alexander the Great, the Seleucid king Antiochus IV defiled the rebuilt temple in 167 B.C. Antiochus determined to stamp out the Hebrew religion. He set up the image of Zeus in the temple and ordered swine sacrificed upon a pagan altar. Jewish outrage at the sacrilege resulted in the successful Maccabean revolt of 164 B.C.

Israel remained independent until 63 B.C., when Jerusalem fell to Pompey's Roman legions. In the years before the birth of Christ, Herod the Great came to power. King Herod was the son of Antipater, a Jew of Arab ancestry and one of Pompey's lieutenants. Herod was cruel, loyal to his Roman masters, and hated by his people. He believed he might win their applause by restoring their modest temple to its former glory.

Herod's restoration was magnificent and a wonder of its day. It was that same splendid temple of Herod, with its massive beautiful stones and majestic buildings, which Jesus's disciples praised as they went out from the temple one day. Jesus responded to his disciples by predicting that not one stone of the temple would be left on another. In 70 A.D., his prophecy was literally fulfilled when the Romans totally destroyed the temple. Not a single stone was left standing. Even the revered "Wailing Wall" in modern day Jerusalem is merely the western retaining wall that supports the platform upon which the temple of Herod was built.

For the next two thousand years the Gentiles would trample the 40 acre temple mount. Since the 8th century, the temple site had been occupied by two of Islam's holiest shrines: the Dome of the Rock and the El Aqsa Mosque. To the Moslem, the holy rock was the spot from which the prophet Mohammed rose upon his horse into heaven.

Realistically, there could be no third temple. Even with the establishment of the state of Israel in 1948, the reconstruction of the temple on Mount Moriah remained a political and practical impossibility. It was the practical problem that was greatly reduced when the two venerable structures, especially the thirteen centuries old Dome, collapsed in a Middle Eastern earthquake. Mason Wolfe would solve the political problem.

Excavation in the area of the mount had caused many scholars to doubt whether the temple's Holy of Holies had formerly been situated directly on the site of the Moslem shrines. Even before the mosques fell, there was a growing consensus that the temple could be rebuilt without the destruction of the shrines. All but the most fervent proponents of the temple recognized, however, that while the Islamic shrines stood, the Arabs would not abide any Jewish construction on the mount, even if the mosques were somehow left intact. The earthquake changed the equation, literally wiping the slate clean, and it was Wolfe that mediated the treaty-guaranteed by the U.N. and the United States of Europe-that would permit the rebuilding of the mosques and the Jewish Temple.

The world was surprised at the speed with which the Israelis raised their new temple. Certain religious groups had long been preparing for the resumption of the temple worship. Priests had trained in the ancient worship and prepared to resume the animal sacrifices that had ceased in 70 A.D. at the destruction of Jerusalem. The sacred vessels and priestly vestments were prepared; the old musical instruments crafted. When—**after** six months—the third temple was dedicated, it was Mason Wolfe who came and spoke to the international audience.

"We now behold the birth of a new age," Wolfe told the world. "What we have done in this hallowed place will be a symbol for our troubled planet. Here Jews and Moslems may worship together. This is as it shall be from this time forward. We now recognize our oneness. We reverence this earth, our mother and source of all life."

The news media reported his words, but it was not exactly Mason Wolfe's words that affected people. It was something else. Orators had been described as spellbinding before, but that misnomer had been used to describe eloquent or sensational speech. To listen to Wolfe was to experience feelings of well-being and belonging. Mason Wolfe was soothing and kind; his words sounded wise and reasonable. To agree with him was to feel oneself wise and reasonable; to disagree seemed vulgar, even ugly. But the magic only worked for the listener. Once committed to print, his words lost their power to move or persuade.

The U.N. Secretary General went beyond his previous offer to resign. He quit unilaterally, in hopes that Wolfe would take the job. A large faction in Israel invited Wolfe to accept Israeli citizenship. Their fervor was not in the least dampened by Wolfe's attenuated Hebrew ancestry, which at best placed his nearest Jewish ancestor more than 1500 years ago. He would be acclaimed Prime Minister, they promised. Wolfe declined all offers; offers to head corporations; offers to head nations; all offers but the last.

So the world was both surprised and delighted when the United States Secretary of State, Mason Wolfe, was appointed as President of the United States of Europe.

Chapter Eight

Clement XV was dead. Just as Cardinal Lindsay had predicted, the fight over succession had begun long before Clement's broken fisherman's ring and papal seals were interred with his body in the crypt of the popes beneath the floor of St. Peter's Basilica.

For centuries the Cardinals of the Church had assembled in Rome to select the next pope in a secretive gathering or "conclave." Now two conclaves moved to grasp the future of the Catholic Church. The smaller of the two had by now come to be known as "the Eight."

Bishop Shea waited with Cardinal Lindsay at the entrance to Cardinal Chiavetta's apartment while being announced by the Florentine Cardinal's secretary, Father Bagnozzi. Chiavetta was the senior member of the Eight and would preside as the Cardinal Camerlengo or Chamberlain of the conclave. Chiavetta had been Clement's most trusted advisor, next to Lombardo. The black-haired Cardinal was once tall and sturdily built, but the years had shrunk his height and widened his girth. Even so, his deep golden voice had only grown in power with every passing year. Guiseppi Chiavetta was that rare man of meek holiness, who nevertheless possessed the

wit and wile of the serpent. Naturally gracious and accom-
modating, the Cardinal Camerlengo could be very intimidating at need.

"Welcome, Eminence!" said the elder man to Lindsay,
"Thank you for coming so quickly after your long journey."

"Let me introduce my auxiliary, Bishop Brendan
Shea."

Chiavetta's eyes narrowed as he looked closely at the
young bishop. "Brendan Shea? I thought you were an American."

"I am an American. You may ask anyone except my
mother. She will insist, however, that I am an Irishman. You
would not want to argue with my mother."

"Except for the accent, I would have to side with your
mother. I look forward to discussing this fellow Mason Wolfe
with you. I have read your report. You have a gift for analyz-
ing facts, Brendan Shea."

"Thank you, Eminence."

"Shall we get down to business?" suggested Chiavetta.
"Seeing Bishop Shea here reminds me of an important issue
as to our conduct of the election. The way I read Clement's
directive, we are bound to elect the next pope by a two thirds'
majority of our eight members. Beyond that single restriction,
we may proceed by any rules that two thirds of us may agree
upon. While I do not propose to relax the secrecy of the conclave, I believe the Church would be better served if each of
us were to bring an assistant to relieve us of some of the work
and to lend their own insights when called upon."

"I agree," replied Lindsay without any hesitation. "I
am sure Bishop Shea would be of great help to me, and, I
think, to my brother Cardinals."

"I have spoken with the others and they too agree,"
said Chiavetta. "It was Lombardo's idea. When we convene
tomorrow we will probably be just 24 hours ahead of the others. They would have elected their 'pope' by now if they had
not been quarreling over us. Even now, there are a dozen who
have refused to come to the other conclave."

"So out of 140 Cardinals, barely twenty will support the new pope?" asked Lindsay.

"No. There are perhaps ten more who are coming to speak against their so-called conclave," answered Chiavetta. "They will support us also. We all know what this dispute is about. It's whether the Church will stand against the waves sweeping over it and the world; or whether She will lie down on the bed prepared for her."

"On what authority do the other Cardinals base their rebellion?" questioned Shea.

"The others are trying to make this into a will contest," responded Chiavetta. "A few of them tried early to claim that Clement's directive was a forgery, but he lived too long after and affirmed the directive in front of too many people for anyone, even the eagerly gullible, to believe such a story. Now most admit it is genuine, but claim that he was deranged when he signed it. Such allegations are baseless. Anyone who knew him, knew also that he was the sanest of men, for he understood both God and man as few men do."

"What can I say of his critics?" Chiavetta continued. "That they cannot see holiness standing before their eyes? I wish that were true, because the truth is worse: they cannot stand holiness before their eyes. No, it is not Clement who was incompetent. The only evidence of his madness is that he loved Christ and the Church, and did his best to preserve the trust now left to us. Despite what they hoped at the time of Clement's election, we all quickly discovered that he was no progressive."

"He was a disappointment to most of our American bishops, who looked to him to make changes and loosen things up," said Lindsay, "With Clement, most American Catholics finally tired of waiting for a pope to their liking and stopped listening to him altogether. Clement became irrelevant to most."

"And one who thumbs his nose at a living pope is not likely to be deterred by a dead one," said Shea.

"True, but now that he is dead they praise him even as they reject his succession directive with their clucking about his 'tragic' mental decline," said Chiavetta.

"Do you believe there will be a schism, then?" Lindsay asked.

"Schism will be the least of it, for the split is not a political feud, but a doctrinal one. Unless the Lord has mercy and shows us a way back to the others, I cannot envision them accepting our choice. We will talk of it when we begin tomorrow. I will be interested in how you, Brendan Shea, see these matters as they relate to the global political situation. Mason Wolfe appears to be the greatest hope this world has seen in two thousand years. Where others have failed, he succeeds. And such a wonder worker! Simon Magus would be jealous. Good night, brothers. Let us be rested for tomorrow."

Lindsay and Shea left Chiavetta and walked to Lindsay's room. Only the Camerlengo enjoyed the luxury of a suite of rooms. Each of the others made do with a simple room equipped with a bed and small writing desk. "What is it you want me to do at the conclave tomorrow? I wasn't expecting to be a participant," said Shea.

"You mean besides praying for a way through this? Don't worry about your part. Just be ready to help me and be ready to speak if you are called upon. We will concelebrate Mass at 6:00 a.m. so I will probably go to sleep soon. If this were any other conclave we would be up half the night attempting to line up support for this position or that candidate. But doubtless this will not be like any other conclave. Every man here appears to be of a similar mind. Clement has seen to that. Each individual elector will likely be an acceptable candidate to each of the others."

"And at the same time likely to be unacceptable to the majority of the Cardinals," added Brendan.

"Yes. Our unity in the conclave is the source of our difficulty."

"Will there be anything else, before I go to my room?" asked Shea.

"No, Brendan. Good night. You know how I value your prayers above all others." Brendan nodded and the Cardinal continued: "Don't leave me out tonight."

"I won't, Eminence. Goodnight," Brendan answered. Brendan let himself out and went to his room to clean up before going to the chapel. As he knelt in the flickering candlelight, Brendan understood the severity of the crisis but at the same time he rested in an inexplicable awareness that the Holy Spirit had taken the initiative. These eight men had only to yield to His will. The Spirit whispered and he understood. Don't strive tomorrow. Don't steer.

Brendan Shea took the long way back to his room and walked slowly through a shadowed garden. The air was cool and every star seemed so real and hard that Brendan felt he must stop to breathe it all in. The idea that the Creator's hand was firmly at the controls was fixed in his mind as he remembered a hymn from the Psalms:

You sit enthroned forever Lord, Your glory never changing.
Your love is endless streaming toward the servants of the king.
He makes the clouds his chariot and rides upon the storm.
He makes the wind his messenger, the flames his servants,
    warm.

After a few moments, Brendan passed on through the garden. He was soon asleep and awakened refreshed despite a short night.

Mass ended before 7:00 a.m. Stewart, the Englishman, caught Lindsay on the way out and invited him and Brendan to have breakfast with himself and his assistant.

"Did Chiavetta speak to you about bringing a second into the conclave?" he said to Lindsay after introductions were made.

"Last night, yes."

"I think he knew you would have young Shea along, so no one bothered to raise the subject with you earlier. Even so, Morumba and Reagan will be alone, unless Scorfazza can get one of them to take him in." Everyone laughed. Cardinal

Scorfazza of Milan was leading the largest faction in the "anti-conclave" as they had begun to call it. Scorfazza's group was united by a single theme: the orthodox Church is out of step with the world. Their spiritual predecessors in an earlier day would have held Marxism in common, but today their association was largely negative.

"Who are the other bishops?" Brendan asked, referring to non-Cardinals at the mass.

"You saw the tiny old Indian with Koomswami? That was Bishop Shopra, Koomswami's professor from the seminary. The bishop is 93 years old. The Indians say he will live forever. Then there is Cardinal Reyes' auxiliary Fernando. He may be as young as you, Bishop Shea."

"And what of Lombardo? There was no one with him at Mass," noted Lindsay.

"Nobody knows. Only Chiavetta has talked with him and Chiavetta doesn't know either," explained Stewart, "In this city, he is wise to keep it a secret till the very last moment." Stewart looked at his watch, then added, "Which I believe is now." The four men rose together and made their way up to the Sistine Chapel.

As they halted before the great door, Brendan Shea quickly took in the scene: Lombardo and Chiavetta were arguing loudly with several Cardinals whom Brendan did not know. Morumba, Koomswami and Reyes looked on bewildered. Reagan came up just behind Stewart and Lindsay. Everything was bathed in lights while television cameras lapped up the discord. Armed Swiss Guards stood unmoving on either side of the quarreling Cardinals. A previously unseen Cardinal stepped forward from the midst of the group and faced Chiavetta.

"Have the 'Eight' decided to obey the Church's summons to this conclave, Lord Chiavetta?" questioned Scorfazza with mock politeness. "If so, I suggest you come back tomorrow when the conclave begins." The Camerlengo bristled, his overgrown eyebrows projecting even further than usual.

"I am here by order of Clement XV, as are these men with me. We, and we alone, shall elect the next successor to St. Peter. I have ordered the Chapel emptied and secured," replied Chiavetta.

"You may have so ordered, but you and your renegade band will not enter here today. We take no orders from Clement's dead hand," Scorfazza said, extending his arms to further block the way. Scorfazza motioned to the guards and the splendidly uniformed men-at-arms formed a barrier against the Eight with Scorfazza at their center. The Eight were clearly overmatched, but did not immediately yield. Then Lombardo spoke quietly for a moment in Chiavetta's ear. Chiavetta nodded and both men turned about and walked out. The balance of the Eight and their assistants followed, brushing past reporters shouting questions, leaving the field to a triumphant Scorfazza.

The thirteen men, led by Lombardo, marched outdoors and had begun to cross a square, when perhaps two dozen guards appeared, not pikemen, but men with firearms. Brendan watched as the Swiss Guards quickly mustered in front of them; their colorful formation blocking the Cardinals' path. Behind, Brendan saw the squad from the Sistine Chapel had now blocked their retreat. Most of the thirteen pulled up short, but Lombardo did not break his stride. The Camerlengo quickly resumed his pace at the side of Lombardo. They did not stop until standing face to face with the unflinching guards.

Each end of the armed line swung around the thirteen until they were completely surrounded. Brendan saw them draw their weapons. Their captain stepped forward. His expression was grim as he looked first to the thirteen, then to his own men and to the following force from the Chapel. Suddenly, he turned his fierce eyes downward and fell to one knee at Chiavetta's feet, announcing:

"My Lord Camerlengo, we are in danger here. My men and I know that the Church of Christ rests in your hands. We are pledged to serve you and the man you will select." The captain rose. "Cardinal Fiore directed me to find you and bring you to the Apostolic Palace. He has prepared a place for the conclave. Please follow me." They listened to the captain and looked to Chiavetta and Lombardo.

"Yes, follow him. Fiore is with us," said Lombardo. The captain led the thirteen to the palace while most of the guard brought up the rear. Along the way Brendan saw more sentries keeping watch along the inside corridors. A few minutes later they were escorted into a large space, which seemed to have been hastily prepared. Furniture had been pushed to one end of the room and a number of tables gathered together to form one large linen-covered conference table. Lombardo presented Cardinal Fiore, Clement's Secretary of State, and Lombardo's colleague in the Conclave. Some were surprised, yet pleased, that Fiore had not joined Scorfazza.

The doors were locked and the guards posted outside. The Camerlengo led the men in prayer and spoke first.

"I would like to begin by asking the eight Cardinals whether they are in agreement that these additional men shall attend this conclave as non-voting members and be bound by the same oath of secrecy."

"Yes," said Lombardo. Koomswami joined him and then each of the others agreed.

"Our brother, Cardinal Stewart, has asked to begin by raising some preliminary questions," Chiavetta announced.

"Thank you, Eminence," Stewart began, "Our experience this morning bears out what we all knew: we are faced with a great crisis; one greater than the Protestant revolt; greater than the Greek Schism. We face the possibility that by the time we leave these rooms neither the Holy Father, nor we will be in unity with nearly a billion Catholics. No elaboration of that disaster is necessary. We must consider alternatives to that likely result."

"Absolutely," said Cardinal Reagan, "We must find another way. We must not allow, we cannot allow, this schism to occur. What alternatives do you propose?"

"First, there is the view of Cardinal Scorfazza and the others," said Stewart. "The issue has been raised that Clement was mad when he chose this course. If that is true, our quandary is solved, because this assembly is illegitimate and we have no choice but to turn aside and join our brother Cardinals."

"Nay," said Morumba as several others shook their heads in agreement with the African.

"But answer this," continued Stewart, "Would the Holy Spirit not guide the entire College as He has throughout the ages?"

"Yes," said Reagan, "for the Spirit is with us always." Brendan winced at Reagan's remarks, surprised at his easy dismissal of Clement's directive.

"What the Holy Spirit might do once we have demonstrated our disobedience is not our concern today," Chiavetta said sharply.

"Is there anyone who counsels that action?" asked Stewart, momentarily ignoring the Camerlengo's rebuke. Stewart stopped and waited for a response. None came. He looked to Reagan, but the Cardinal was silent and held his tongue for the moment. "Good," said Stewart. "Nor do I."

"But there may be other ways out of our dilemma." It was Reagan speaking again. "We must elect a Pontiff for the whole Church. If we elect a man agreeable to the majority of Cardinals, we may yet head off the split."

"But who could that person be?" asked Cardinal Morumba, "Certainly no one in this room!"

"The Code of Canon Law does not limit candidates to the electors themselves," said Lindsay, who was recognized as the premier canon lawyer in the conclave. "The man need not even be a bishop. But beyond the legal question I wonder how our predecessors have dealt with this issue." Lindsay looked at Brendan Shea, seated at his right. "Bishop Shea keeps my history book in his head. What do you say, Brendan?"

Brendan was reluctant to speak among these giants of the Church and demurred: "I am no canon lawyer."

"Yes, but I know no better Church historian," countered Lindsay.

Brendan acquiesced and started to speak. "I know of nothing to suggest that the selection must be limited to the electors themselves. Obviously you may elect any Cardinal. Conclaves have reached even further for candidates."

"In the 13th century a conclave of just eleven Cardinals were deadlocked. For more than two years they fought and failed to complete their task of electing a new pope. King Charles II of Naples came to Rome and suggested that the Cardinals should finish their job. They dismissed the king as a meddling layman and advised him to mind his own business. As the king rode back to Naples he paid a visit to an old and well known hermit named Peter who lived in a cave on Mount Murrone. After the king's visit Peter did a very un-hermit-like thing. He composed a letter chastising the Cardinals, and warning them to fulfill their duty and elect a pope. The letter came into the hands of one Cardinal who produced it at an especially heated moment in the conclave. He read the letter and immediately announced his intention to vote for Peter of Murrone for pope. Peter was unanimously elected pope and was summoned from his cave to serve as Pope Celestine V."

"Well then, we have a free hand. Where is our Peter Murrone?" said the Filipino, Cardinal Reyes, laughing.

"I should add that Celestine appointed enough extra Cardinals to facilitate the next election and then resigned his office after five months," Brendan said.

"That raises an interesting idea," said Stewart. "We all know it is unlikely the College would accept anyone that we elect. We might, however, fulfill our oath and our duty by electing one of our own number. If he were then to re-instate papal selection by the entire College of Cardinals, he could resign and return to his cave."

Brendan jumped in before he could stop himself, "Pardon Eminence, but Peter Celestine did not go back to his cave. The new pope put him in jail where he later died."

"I think that just raises another problem, brothers." Koomswami spoke for the first time. "Cardinal Stewart's solution is a balm to seven of us, but one of us would have to play Peter Celestine. I challenge each of you: Would you dare commit yourself to this course before election? Such a promise could not bind the new pope once he is pope. He may honor the commitment or he may not. Such a promise is not possible on this side of the divide. My counsel is to dispense with these sophistic games—which only tempt us to disobedience—and get on with our task. We have all rejected the notion that Clement was mad. That done, I suggest that we listen to him."

The Indian took out his glasses. "See what he wrote: *'Many of the shepherds have become wolves among the sheep. And the sheep suffer . . . They ask why His Vicar does not remove the wolf and the thief from the sheep pen . . . . Meanwhile, the wolf is emboldened to plunder still more. I have attempted to remove the wolf from the pen, but the Spirit would not permit it.'*" Koomswami, looking up, removed his glasses and repeated, "*'The Spirit would not permit it.'* I believe that if we fulfill our oath straight away, the Spirit himself will allow that which He would not permit Clement to do. It may be God's will that the wolf remove himself. Please Professor Shopra, I think it is time we give voice to our private conclusions."

The ancient bishop nodded and rose at his place. "I have prayed that I would die before seeing this day, but I am still here and now the darkness may be upon us. It is time we consider the possibility that this crisis we face, indeed, the very crisis we are about to precipitate, is the great apostasy that must come over the earth before the great and terrible day of the Lord."

"Bishop Shopra, have you considered how many fanatics have wasted their lives chasing after such ideas?" challenged Reagan.

"Saint Martin of Tours was such a fanatic," said Shopra. "Saint Norbert and Saint Vincent Ferrer too. Pope Saint Gregory the Great was convinced that the reign of antichrist was near at hand."

"Yes, and they were all wrong. Such talk can only distract us from our task," Reagan insisted. "Does not the scripture tell us that no one knows the day or hour?"

"And because we cannot know, we are told to watch and be ready," said Shopra. "Far from distracting the Church from her mission in the world, the anticipation of the Lord's coming commits her to it all the more strongly."

"I must agree with Bishop Shopra," said Chiavetta. "We must always be mindful that ours may be the generation that sees the Lord's return. Our situation is unique in history. The times are extraordinary. And there is more here than the growing apostasy. This man Mason Wolfe has been much on my mind and some of you may be aware that Bishop Shea has followed Wolfe's activities for many years."

Many in the room shifted uncomfortably in their chairs. Reagan impatiently tossed his pen across the table. Morumba shook his head as if pained to listen to what Chiavetta was saying.

Chiavetta continued, "I think we would profit from Bishop Shea's insights regarding the new President of the United States of Europe." Chiavetta leaned back and gestured for Brendan to rise.

Brendan stood at his place and started at the beginning. He told of his first encounter with the state senator Wolfe and Wolfe's rise in American politics. He spoke of the Kansas City bombing and Wolfe's seemingly miraculous escape. Lindsay made certain that Brendan told the full story of the hospital. No other Cardinal interrupted. The Cardinals listened to Lindsay's auxiliary to learn what they might of the enigmatic Mason Wolfe, but most could not but wonder even more about this young bishop who had not only healed the sick, but raised the dead. They had all seen Wolfe on television; seen how he commanded every situation; seen how men would not only kill for him; but even more telling, how they would lay down their arms for him. Yet the unshakable Wolfe was unnerved by the mere sight of Brendan Shea.

The Cardinals nodded as Shea reviewed Wolfe's recent rise to power and details of the latest events in the Middle East. He reminded the Cardinals of Wolfe's claim of Jewish descent from the family of Christ and the House of David through the Merovingian kings. "Another Jewish ancestral line claims Wolfe's descent from the tribe of Dan," Brendan told them. "From Dan, say the early Church fathers, will come the man of sin, the antichrist."

"If I may mention one other thing," interrupted Cardinal Lindsay. "I think everyone here has heard of the apparition that appeared near my city of St. Louis just six months ago. You are also aware of the message the lady brought and the sign that she promised. Considering recent events, especially those following the Kansas City bombing, it seems that Mason Wolfe is the one she spoke of as her son."

"Yes, we have all heard quite enough about 'the Lady,' Eminence," said Reagan. "It has been obvious from the first that the children were lying. Add to that an earthquake that had been expected for at least a hundred years and the sum is still zero, my brothers. Since when have we given honor to false apparitions?"

"No one has said anything about honoring her," said Brendan Shea, "for the lady was false, I am sure. But the children did not lie. If you had seen the bright vision and then moments later seen a great volcano born from the very spot, you would not doubt it either."

"But I did not," said Reagan.

"But I did," Brendan said. "I was there and I saw her with my own eyes. She was not from heaven."

Brendan sat down. Reagan was unmoved.

"Bishop Shea," said Reagan, "Many believe that the spirit of antichrist is the principle of evil in the world. Does not the scripture tell us that the antichrist is he who denies that Jesus Christ has come in the flesh? Certainly there have been men who were types of antichrist, but can we say without doubt that antichrist is an individual man; an individual man who comes at a particular time, perhaps even this time, Bishop Shea?"

"Eminence, the judgment of the Church fathers and tradition has always been in general agreement that the antichrist will be a flesh and blood man. The scriptures, both the Old Testament and the New, speak of a man who will rule over the earth, doing marvelous things and making himself out to be as God.

"The *Didache* or Teachings of the Twelve Apostles tell us that 'in the last days there shall appear the deceiver of the world as a Son of God, and he shall do signs and wonders and the earth shall be given over into his hands and he shall commit iniquities which have never been since the world began.' St. Irenaeus taught that antichrist would be a man. So did Cyril of Jerusalem, St. Augustine and Pope St. Gregory the Great. John Henry Newman, that great mind of the nineteenth century, was led by scripture, the Fathers and the tradition of the Church to conclude that antichrist will certainly be a man."

"Let us assume for a moment the correctness of that view," responded Reagan. "Can we be so arrogant as to believe that we are living in the time of the Second Coming and to declare that this Mason Wolfe is now or will be revealed as the antichrist of which you speak?"

Brendan did not look at Reagan but kept his eyes downcast. He had not found his own words especially convincing, but he did not doubt the conclusion. "Yes," Brendan answered quietly.

Koomswami stood. "In the last days God will permit a powerful delusion so that men will believe the lies of Satan. Now in our midst, that delusion is at work; blinding us to the great apostasy, which has eaten all but a remnant of the Church. Our Protestant brothers and the eastern Churches—in the shortest space of time—have largely forsaken the teachings of scripture that for centuries united us as Christians. We Eight, who represent that faithful remnant, must choose whether the remnant will join the apostasy. Brother Cardinals, shall we now dissolve the Church of Christ on earth? Never, brothers, for that is impossible! Speak now if you believe we can choose anyone but God's man in this terrible hour; the man who Christ has brought to this place to bear His cross as champion of the people of God!"

Brendan had remained with eyes down and praying that the Spirit's hand would remain. Now he looked up as if expecting Christ's champion to break through the locked doors and be revealed.

"The hand of the Lord is on his chosen," continued Koomswami, "and I intend to cast my vote for this man, Brendan Shea."

"I second the nomination of Bishop Shea." It was Lindsay. Brendan turned to his left shaking his head and grasping Lindsay's arm.

"I cannot believe you are serious," said Reagan as he swung around behind his chair. Reagan held out his arm toward Brendan and extended his finger. "Look at him," he shouted. Reagan grimaced as he searched for words. "You cannot be even forty years old!"

"I too will vote for Bishop Shea," said Morumba. Cardinal Reyes nodded his agreement, followed by Lombardo. Five votes. One more would exceed the two-thirds requirement.

Their eyes fell to Stewart who appeared to be making some notes to himself. Stewart put down the pen and peacefully said, "Yes, Brendan Shea is the man."

Reagan said nothing, but turned for the nearest door. His anger flashed when the locked door would not open and he brought a heavy fist onto the center of the door. "Open this now!" shouted the Cardinal. The guards outside were startled and could be heard scrambling to get the door open and to find what was the matter inside. The Camerlengo came to Reagan's side before the door came open, but Reagan turned away as the door swung open. The Camerlengo motioned to the guard not to hinder Reagan and the Cardinal strode out and disappeared.

Chiavetta directed the room to be resealed and the men resumed their seats. "Is there a need for a secret ballot?" asked Chiavetta smiling. "Is there another nomination?" No one spoke.

"Then I ask that each of the seven Cardinals signify by his 'yea' or 'nay' whether he casts his vote for Brendan Shea." One by one the Cardinals spoke their vote for Brendan. Finally, the vote came to the Camerlengo. Chiavetta walked around the table and stood next to Brendan.

"Yea," said Chiavetta and then looking down at Shea he spoke the traditional question: "*Acceptasne fieri in Romanum Pontificem?*" Do you accept to be made pope?

Brendan was bent with his hands over his head, face down to the table, his coarse red hair poking between the fingers of his clasped hands. "Dear God, until this moment it seemed plain that your spirit was upon this election," he prayed silently. Had any man, Brendan wondered, been offered such a cup as this? Impossible it seemed to him, yet he felt the Lord's hand in it. Brendan sat back. The Camerlengo laid his hand on Brendan's shoulder and Brendan stood up. No man ever felt less sufficient to the task.

"I do," said Brendan Shea. Lindsay turned and embraced the new Pope and spoke closely.

"This is meant for you Brendan."

The Camerlengo and each of the others likewise embraced the new pope speaking words of encouragement. "You will not bear the burden alone," said Stewart, "What can we do to serve you and the Church of Christ?"

"Please. Let's go back to the table," Brendan asked the Cardinals as he returned to his own chair. "Cardinal Chiavetta, Cardinal Lombardo, you understand better than anyone what is occurring outside as our brothers are preparing to elect another man. What must we do now and during the next twenty-four hours?" Brendan twisted around to look to each corner of the room and a smile formed momentarily. "Even if we had the customary ballots to burn, there does not appear to be any stove at hand in which to burn them," he joked. "It seems no white smoke will announce my election."

Lombardo answered, "Cardinal Fiore knows how hastily this room was prepared, Holiness." Fiore nodded pleasantly and Lombardo continued, "But the question of how to announce your election is one we must consider carefully. The anti-conclave will commence tomorrow morning. I think there should be an immediate public announcement before the others meet."

"No," Brendan said. "I'm not comfortable with by-passing the Cardinals, however hostile they may be. Can you arrange for me to address them in the morning?"

"They will not accept you," said Chiavetta.

"Some will. At any rate, every man of them must be given the choice. After I have faced the College, then I will go to the people. Can we do it?"

"I think so," said Lombardo. "If our choice had been one of the Eight, I would say no. But they will be curious about you. Curious enough to let you speak before they reject you."

"Perhaps they will not reject our new pope," said Cardinal Koomswami. "We have today learned how the Holy Spirit leads where no one expects to go. Who can say what our brother Bishops will do?"

"Yes, Cardinal. Who can say?" Brendan said. "Meanwhile we have a few things to think about. And pray about."

Brendan awoke the next morning. He had no clothes, except those he had brought with him, and he tried to remember when the pope was supposed to put on the white robe. No matter, for this morning the Bishop of Rome would dress as the auxiliary Bishop of the Archdiocese of St. Louis, Missouri.

The tense moments with the guards the previous morning came back to him when he left his room to seek out Cardinal Lindsay. A pair of Swiss Guards had accompanied Brendan to the room the prior evening, but it had not occurred to him that they would not move from his door during the night. He walked the short distance to Lindsay's room and Lindsay greeted him at the door.

"Good morning, Holiness," Lindsay said to him.

Brendan raised his hand, "Please, you are a father to me and I would like to remain Brendan to you."

"Alright Brendan, but by what name will the world remember you."

Brendan had guessed Lindsay would demand the new name. Like Simon the fisherman, the newest Vicar of Christ customarily took a new name to acknowledge his new place between heaven and earth. Brendan had been shaving just thirty minutes before when he realized he did not want a new name. He had first been called to the priesthood as Brendan and Brendan he would remain.

"Brendan," he said.

"Brendan the First," said Lindsay aloud, trying the sound in his mind and in his ear. "And the last, perhaps."

Lindsay and Brendan joined the rest of the "Eight" for Mass, but Cardinal Reagan did not attend. The group met briefly after in Chiavetta's rooms then followed Chiavetta and Brendan to the Sistine Chapel.

When they arrived the guards at the door immediately admitted them to the chapel where their brother Cardinals had commenced opening remarks in the "anti-conclave." Brendan's guard remained outside uneasily with Scorfazza's men-at-arms. Lombardo scowled as he noticed that a dozen or so Cardinals seated near the front of the group were not Cardinals at all, but women, dressed as Cardinals, having been invited as observers to the conclave.

Cardinal Scorfazza was outlining the sequence of speakers for the morning and was preparing to give the floor to Cardinal Reagan, apparently so that Reagan might bring the Cardinals up to date regarding the events of the previous day's election. Reagan had risen and walked to Scorfazza's side, when Scorfazza saw Brendan's group enter. Scorfazza stopped as every eye watched Chiavetta approach Scorfazza.

"We have a pope," said the Camerlengo to Scorfazza quietly, "and he wishes to address the assembly."

"We know what you have done," replied Scorfazza. "Your Bishop Shea will be given a hearing if that is his request." Scorfazza started to step to the microphone, but Chiavetta moved ahead of him and gained the floor.

"Eminences," Chiavetta began. His sonorous voice heightened each Cardinal's attention, even though he spoke quietly. "Yesterday the eight Cardinals designated by Clement XV met in conclave. We have chosen Clement's successor. He is Bishop Brendan Shea." He turned to Brendan and raising his voice, Chiavetta announced, "Pope Brendan the First."

The great room remained silent as Brendan stepped to the microphone. Then he began: "Peace to all of you, my brothers in Jesus Christ. I came to this city by the side of Cardinal Lindsay, from St. Louis in the United States. Although few of you have even heard of me, I stand before you today as your Pope." Grunts and sneers among the Cardinals. The nuns giggled.

"Are you going to resign so that a united Church may choose our new pope?" interrupted Reagan loudly, still near the podium.

"No. The choice is the Lord's. The burden is mine. I ask you to set aside the divisions that have driven us apart."

The "Eight" minus Reagan stepped toward the pope and each went down on a knee. Then Rodriguez of Los Angeles left his seat and walked slowly to where the Pope stood. He reached Brendan, knelt and laid his red cap at his feet. Then the Frenchman Roulle and a dozen others quietly left their places and came humbly forward. Scorfazza abruptly took the microphone from Brendan.

"My brothers, this is no time for unconsidered action. I ask you to retake your seats." No one else rose, but none returned to his place either. "We now stand on the edge of a precipice. For too long the Church has been smothered by a medieval clique that now offers us this man Shea; this young man who is obviously a puppet doing their will. But their time draws to a close." Scorfazza became more scornful as he spoke.

"Brendan Shea begs us to set aside our divisions, but we have heard that plea from them before. 'Let us come together, brothers,'" Scorfazza mocked. "Coming together has but one meaning for them: 'bend the knee, and follow thou me.' No Brendan Shea. No, dear Camerlengo. We do not submit. No longer will a tiny minority rule the vast majority who make up the body of Christ. What rotten arrogance! What spiritual pride has eaten the hearts and shriveled the souls of these little men? Their only solution is to turn back the clock, to turn from the future, in a forced march, nay my brothers and sisters, a death march, to the past."

"But that is not the way!" Scorfazza continued. "No, our way is forward. Now let us trust in Christ and go forward with confidence that the Spirit of God leads us. Let us believe that the Holy Spirit can unite us all in love. Will you trust Christ? Will you trust Christ and go forward?"

Scorfazza stopped a moment and conferred with a monsignor who seemed to nod toward a pair of screens set up at each end of the chapel.

Then Scorfazza, now grave, continued: "There is something that gives me no pleasure to convey, but it must be said. Brendan Shea is not only a false and illicit pope but we have received information that he is now a fugitive from justice, wanted by the United States for mass murder in the recent bombing in Kansas City."

The room broke out with shouts and loud conversations. Brendan looked toward Chiavetta and the Eight. It was clear he was as surprised at Scorfazza's scandalous announcement as they.

"At this time it is known that Bishop Shea is a long-time anti-abortion radical and confederate of two men now known to be responsible for the bombing. Brothers and Sisters, look to the television monitors."

The previously darkened screens became alive with a news report recorded during the night. The Cardinals watched what appeared to be some sort of anti-abortion protest as the narrator explained: "Four years ago Mason Wolfe was a State Senator in Lexington, Kentucky when he attended a pro-choice dinner at which he was honored. A few anti-abortion extremists gathered outside the banquet to harass the future President of Europe."

"This man," the narrator continued as the camera lingered on one protester's face, "is John Daniels, one of two men now being held without bond on 817 counts of first degree murder." The camera cut to the face of another man wearing a clerical collar, "and this man is Brendan Shea, now Auxiliary Bishop of St. Louis and a leader within an ultraconservative faction of the Catholic Church." The recording ends with the shocked face of Mason Wolfe who is seemingly being accosted by Shea who confronts Wolfe through the window of the Senator's car. Then the monitors went blank.

"Evidence obtained by the American Justice Department, implicates Brendan Shea in the murder of those innocent human beings," Cardinal Scorfazza added, "and he is known to have been in Kansas City in the vicinity of the bombing on that infamous night. I have further information that he is being sought by Italian authorities at this very hour."

As if on cue, the great doors of the Sistine Chapel swung open to reveal turmoil outside the doors equal to that within. Brendan's Swiss Guards burst in and ran forward to surround the pope. A cohort of Italy's special police, the Carabinieri, streamed across the threshold and into the chapel. To Brendan's left, the police used their clubs to cut a path toward him. Two of his guards went down in pain.

The captain of Brendan's guard gave a shout and raising his sidearm above his head, fired a single round into Michaelangelo's Last Judgment. His guard drew their firearms and the police stopped the clubbing and began to unholster their own weapons.

"Stop!" shouted Brendan, standing next to Scorfazza. The room became silent. "What do you want?" he asked. Slowly, from back in the ranks, came the commander of the Carabinieri. Brendan followed him with his eyes until the commander stood before him. The captain stood at the pope's side, ready to die before Brendan should be taken.

"Brendan Shea, I have orders that you are to come with me," the commander said. The captain of the guard leveled his weapon at the commander, but Brendan raised his hand, bringing it down on the captain's gun.

"None of this," he said, "Tell your men to put away their weapons. I will go with the police."

The Carabinieri escorted Brendan out of the chapel. Less than two hours later, the pope had been handed over to four U.S. Marshals and was in a jet on his way to Kansas City.

Chapter Nine

If the federal agents intended to interrogate Brendan, they gave no sign of it during the long flight back to the United States. Except for meals and trips to the restroom, no one spoke to him throughout the trip. The U.S. Attorney had not announced whether federal charges would be brought against the Kansas City bombers. In truth, federal prosecutors were still puzzling about how they might be effectively charged under existing federal law.

Thus the bombers had been charged under Missouri law and Brendan was turned over to Jackson County Sheriff's deputies at the downtown airport. Brendan's legs were shackled and his hands cuffed and fastened to a chain about his waist as he was driven to the county jail. At the jail there were no onlookers, no press. Brendan wondered if anyone besides these lawmen even knew where he was.

Instead of being fingerprinted and photographed he was taken directly to a small courtroom inside the jail itself. He was seated by himself on a long bench. Except for the deputies, the only other person in the courtroom was a middle-aged woman seated at a table near the judge's bench.

"All rise," ordered a deputy as he tugged Brendan to his feet. The judge entered from behind the bench and took his seat.

"Brendan Shea?"

"Yes."

"Please approach the bench," the judge ordered. Brendan shuffled up to the bench, his chains dragging the floor as he moved. "I am Judge Somerson and this is Ms. Byrnes, Jackson County Prosecuting Attorney." Brendan did not appreciate how unusual it was that the chief prosecutor should do anything outside her office without cameras in attendance.

"You are being charged with multiple felony counts and you have the right to an attorney. If you cannot afford an attorney, one will be appointed to represent you. Do you understand?"

"I understand," he answered.

"Since you may be held for some time, you are entitled to a preliminary hearing to determine if there is probable cause to believe that a felony has been committed and probable cause to believe that you are the person who has committed that felony."

The judge began to read from the thick criminal complaint. "The State charges, in Count I, that on the 7th day of April, this year, in the County of Jackson, State of Missouri, you committed the class A felony of murder in the first degree, punishable by death or imprisonment for life, in that you, acting together with others, after deliberation, knowingly killed Governor John P. McDonald with a bomb. In Count II, the State charges . . . ."

The judge stopped. "Is there a public defender still in the building?" One of the deputies left the courtroom. "Have him sit down. I'll be here all night if I have to read all 817 counts of this complaint. We're in recess," the judge said abruptly, then walked out.

Fifteen minutes later, a young woman entered the courtroom. The deputies left her alone with Brendan and she introduced herself as an attorney with the state public defender's office. Brendan told her he would accept whatever help she could give. She explained that she was required to ask him a few questions about his financial ability to hire an attorney and Brendan explained that a Catholic priest, even in America, owned little beyond an automobile and some personal belongings.

"Do you have a job?" she asked. Brendan was amused as he thought about the story this girl would take home this evening.

"I do," he answered. "I'm the Pope."

Brendan watched her write "Pope" on the application. "How much money do you earn?"

"I'm not sure. I just took the job and haven't got my first paycheck."

"Are you really the Pope?" she said eyeing him and suspecting a joke was being played on her.

"Yes, I really am. But I doubt if the Church is going to be supporting me at all." She seemed satisfied and left to tell the prosecutor and judge that she was ready. Everyone returned to the courtroom.

"Have you had time to speak with the defendant?" asked the judge, speaking to Brendan's attorney.

"Yes. He qualifies for our services. I will enter my appearance on his behalf. We waive formal reading of the complaint and ask this case be continued for two weeks."

"Case continued two weeks. The prisoner will be held without bond." The judge left the bench.

Brendan's attorney told him an attorney from the Capital Crimes Unit of the Public Defender's office would soon replace her. Brendan was removed from the courtroom, escorted to the jail proper, and after booking, placed in a cell. Except for the camera across the hall, he was finally alone.

The next day Henry Gonzales visited Brendan during lunch. Gonzales stayed long enough to explain that he would take over Brendan's case from the young attorney and that Brendan should say nothing about his case to anyone. Brendan told him that since he knew nothing about his case he would have no problem keeping quiet about it.

Brendan's cell had been designed for more than one prisoner and he observed it was not much smaller than the room he had stayed in at Rome two nights before. The food was adequate and since Gonzales had been his only interruption, he found he had unlimited time to pray. But with so much time to spare, he was reminded how quickly one ran out of to things to say to God: things to be sorry for, things to be thankful for, things to ask for. So Brendan prayed more to listen than to inform.

His custom had been to pray the Liturgy of the Hours or the "Divine Office," those prayers and scripture readings designed to be read at certain times of the day, but he did not have his books. They had even taken away his rosary. Brendan might use it to hang himself, the jailer had explained. Ten fingers would have to do.

The second night in jail he woke in the middle of the night to the sound of another prisoner shouting for a deputy. Brendan found his own bed soaked through with water. Soon a jailer came through and announced that a water pipe had broken and it would be necessary to move some people around. Brendan was taken to another wing where he found he would be sharing quarters. His cellmate did not stir as Brendan climbed into the upper bunk. It was dry and Brendan was soon asleep.

Brendan was awakened by the sound of his cellmate using the toilet. He lay in the bunk and silently said his morning prayers. His time of solitude had been short, but then he had not set out to be a monk, he thought, but a parish priest. Brendan turned over and looked at the other man.

"Good morning, I'm Brendan Shea."

"I didn't expect to see anyone in here this morning," said the other man as he lay back down in the lower bunk. "I haven't had company since I got here." The man was not unfriendly, but seemed very sad. Brendan said nothing more until the jailer brought breakfast.

The man's name was John and he was awaiting trial. Judging from the length of his stay Brendan decided that

John must be accused of a serious crime, but neither of the two men immediately offered an account of how they came to be in the jail.

During the day, John discovered that an empty cell next to his had also been occupied during the night. They could not see the young man in the next cell but it was apparent to Brendan that John knew the neighbor. Meanwhile, Brendan studied his new roommate. It took him until after dinner that night before he finally settled his mind that he had seen John before.

"You were injured in the Royal Regency Bombing, weren't you?"

"Why do you ask?" John had been sternly warned by his attorney not to speak to anyone about the bombing. John had thought the warnings rather foolish since John had confessed his own involvement within hours of his arrest. His public defender never tired of telling him there was no point in having an attorney if you weren't going to listen to his advice.

"I was there at Downtown Hospital that night," Brendan explained, "and I believe you were too. Only I recall that you were in bad shape that night, but you seem to be in fine health now."

"Except that I could use a little more sun than I get these days," John said, smiling grimly. "I am told that my emergency room chart showed me with serious burns over half my body. Yet they discharged me the next day. The police caught up with me at my apartment wanting to talk. I signed a consent to search and thirty minutes later my computer and I were at the station. I gave them a written statement. Now here I am, charged with 817 counts of first degree murder. I'm guilty of every one of them."

"Do you know what happened to you at the hospital that night?" Brendan asked. John seemed surprised that Brendan had made no reaction to his stark confession. While Brendan was wearing the same bright orange jumpsuit as his cellmate, John could not guess that Brendan's job description had long included listening to the shocking admissions of his fellow men.

"I was healed as if by a miracle," said John. "As hard as it is to believe, it seems certain that Mason Wolfe had something to do with it. I was not the only one healed, you know."

"You are not a Catholic, are you?"

"No."

"Then I have a confession of sorts to make to you," Brendan said. "I was at the hospital that night, as a kind of emergency chaplain."

"You are a Catholic priest, I take it?"

"I hope you don't mind, but not knowing your religion, I was given an opportunity to give you the last rites of the Church. Under the circumstances, you might say I decided to anoint first and ask questions later."

"I don't suppose it 'takes' unless you are Catholic," John replied and then changed the subject. "I don't think they get many priests on this side of the bars. Why are you here, Brendan . . . or is it Father Brendan?"

"Call no one on earth 'Father,'" came a voice from the new prisoner in the next cell, "for you have one Father who is in heaven. Matthew 23, verse 9."

"Be quiet Jimmy," John said.

"Brendan would be fine," said the Pope.

The next day John's mood seemed to brighten and he began to take an interest in Brendan. John pressed Brendan for his story and so spent the morning listening to the pope's tale. Jimmy listened too, but nothing could temper Jimmy's contempt. He would shout accusations against the Catholic Church, calling it the "Whore of Babylon." When Brendan reached the place in the story where he was elected pope, Jimmy immediately declared him to be the antichrist.

"If you are who you say you are, then you should be able get us out of here!"

"Shut up, Jimmy!" John came back in rebuke, "We deserve to be here, but you and I both know that this man is completely innocent. So leave him alone."

Jimmy spoke no more to John or Brendan, but could frequently be heard muttering, even cursing, and sometimes quoting scripture.

Aside from their criminal charges, Brendan and John had few other interests in common and so frequently turned to issues of religion; and more often than not, the differences between John's evangelical Christianity and the Catholicism of Brendan. Brendan spent a great deal of time answering John's objections to the Catholic faith. Brendan was successful in helping John to understand the Catholic view of things, but in the end the issues always came down to whose interpretation was correct. Eventually, Brendan persuaded John to temporarily set aside his specific objections to the Church long enough to consider the broader issue of authority.

"It is a curious thing about how the Protestant churches regard the Catholic Church. It would make a little one act play," Brendan said, getting John's interest.

"Let's set the scene in a great European cathedral during Martin Luther's revolt. The Protestants storm the sanctuary. After booting out the priest, they overturn and begin to break up the altar. Two of them set about taking down the great crucifix. They chop it into firewood and throw it onto the broken altar. One gathers up the candles; another the priests' vestments. A fire is lit. Do you get the idea, John? What else for the fire?"

John decided to play along, "Are there statues in the church?"

"Lots," answered Brendan, "And confessionals too."

"What?"

"Little booths where the priest hears confessions."

"OK, it's all on the fire, what's next?" said John.

"By this time the great church is nearly stripped; the beautiful stained glass windows shattered. The fire is blazing halfway to the high ceiling. Only the pews and the pulpit remain. Suddenly one of the frenzied reformers takes hold of the scriptures atop the pulpit. He prances toward the flames with the Bible held high, but just before he tosses it on, one of his reformer friends screams 'Stop!' and they all gather around the man. They take the book from him and curiously turn it over, examining it carefully. The chief reformer takes it, now holding it out with both hands, and solemnly declares, 'This is the Word of the Lord.' Then he invites each man to come forward and each kisses the book."

John was still turning the picture around in his mind. He could not quite see where Brendan was going with it. Brendan continued.

"And thus one object survives the reformers' purge and becomes the center of worship and life in the revolutionary church. What's the point of the story, John?"

"The point is that the Catholic Church has added on all sorts of doctrines and practices that are nowhere found in the New Testament. We must return to the Bible; the Bible alone."

"The Bible? Where do you get the New Testament, John? You get it from the same place you got the confessional, the candles, the incense and the altar. You got it from the Catholic Church and you haven't the slightest reason to believe a single word in it, except that the Catholic Church has told you it is the very Word of God. The New Testament was written, assembled, and preserved by and upon the authority of the Catholic Church. I don't quite see how you can reverence the Bible and yet disregard the other Traditions of the Church. Both the Bible and the Church's other teachings stand on the same foundation. If you reject the Catholic Church you saw off the branch your Bible is sitting on."

John took it all in respectfully, but gave no indication that his personal catechesis by the Vicar of Christ was having any effect on his thoroughly Protestant mind. Brendan did not press the discussion further. The two men were eating lunch the next day when John set down his fork to question Brendan.

"Mason Wolfe did not heal me that night, did he?" he said. "You did."

"Not me. God healed you."

"Yes, but when you gave me the anointing . . . ."

Brendan nodded.

"Then I believe that you are who you say you are. You are Christ's man on earth and I will follow you. What must I do to be saved?"

It would take time for John to understand, but Brendan was willing to accept John's imperfect personal allegiance. Brendan heard his confession and John was surprised when Brendan produced unleavened bread and wine for mass and John's first Communion. John mentioned that even in jail Brendan must have many friends near at hand, but Brendan did not know who had substituted wine in his half-pint of milk. The bread, however, was no mystery as Brendan had saved a package of crackers from his dinner.

It was evening when the call came from Cardinal Lindsay. Lindsay had only days before returned from the conclave in Rome, where Lindsay and the Eight had publicly announced the election of Pope Brendan I. Lindsay had not stayed for the election of Cardinal Scorfazza, now styled "Pope John XXIV." Bertoldi had watched the media reports that were favoring Scorfazza as the new pope.

Tom Bertoldi had not known that Brendan was being quietly held in the Jackson County jail. Lindsay intended to ask a favor.

"I hope you are enjoying your new assignment, Tom," said the Cardinal.

"There wasn't room for both me and the Lady in River Bend."

"Or anyone else," added the Cardinal. "We're still dusting the ashes off the Cathedral here. Listen, Tom. Brendan Shea was validly elected. He is now charged with murders he had nothing to do with. I've only just learned that he is being held in a Kansas City jail. We have to help him and I am powerless here. Already Scorfazza has cut off my access to funds."

"OK, Michael. What can I do from here?"

"You can't do it from there. Brendan has many friends outside official channels and already there is a substantial sum available for his defense. What I need is for you to drive to Kansas City. Do not tell anyone where you are going. I have the name of an attorney there and I want you to hire him. I don't even think this fellow does much criminal defense work, but he will want to help and he will know where to find other help."

Early the next morning, the Cardinal's courier arrived on Father Bertoldi's doorstep and turned over a generous sum of money for the defense of Pope Brendan. Bertoldi called Joseph Dupre's office and obtained an afternoon appointment, then prayed that his old car would make the five-hour drive.

Bertoldi sat patiently as he shared the 20th floor waiting room with a graying couple. The lawyer's secretary had apologized that Mr. Dupre was running late after lunch, so Bertoldi was forced to endure the bickering pair. The man was insistent that their pot-smoking 30 year-old musician son be cut out of their wills. The woman cried and then tried to enlist Bertoldi on her side of the argument, but the priest managed to stay out of the fray. Father Bertoldi wondered how Joseph Dupre, attorney at law, would react to Bertoldi's request.

"Mr. Bertoldi? Mr. Dupre can see you now."

"Please sit down, Father," invited the short, fifty year old attorney. "I understand you are in town from St. Louis?"

"Near St. Louis, Mr. Dupre."

"Call me Joe. You are here about a criminal matter, is that right?"

Bertoldi took more than his allotted half-hour, but Joe kept asking questions, most of which the priest could not answer. Bertoldi understood, however, why Lindsay had recommended this man. Clearly Dupre knew his business and Bertoldi gladly unburdened himself of Brendan's legal problems. But further, Joseph Dupre was a son of the Church, one who listened when the Church spoke, and would not hear what the Church proclaimed false. And he did not need to be convinced that Brendan was Pope.

"You know I am not really a criminal defense attorney," Dupre said, "but let's go talk to him, and then we'll see. I know a dozen defense attorneys who will help when the time comes." Dupre got up and Bertoldi followed.

"Call my four o'clock and see if we can reschedule," he said to the secretary. "You have a car here, Father?"

"In the parking garage."

"If you'll drive, I'll give directions. The jail is not far."

After ten minutes of stoplights and late afternoon traffic, Joe directed the priest to a final right turn onto the street that the jail was on. Joe Dupre proved an excellent guide to the county jail, but now seemed a bit at a loss as to where Father Bertoldi might park the car.

"This is Henry Gonzales, public defender's office. I need to speak to Miriam Byrnes right now."

"I'm sorry but Ms. Byrnes is in a meeting," replied the receptionist at the Jackson County Prosecutor's office.

"I need to talk to her now. It's about Brendan Shea, John Daniels and Jimmy Anderson," insisted Gonzales.

"Please hold a minute, Mr. Gonzales."

Brendan was reading when the messenger came. He did not see the door swing open, nor see the man walk in. He was just there. Brendan sat up, looked at the man and the open door, then jumped down from the top bunk. From the bunk, Brendan had not appreciated the man's size, but now he saw a towering seven foot goliath.

"Quickly. We must go," the angel said to him. The creature motioned toward John. "He can come too, if he will." John still lay on the bottom bunk with his stereo headphones shutting out the world. Brendan shook him and John opened his eyes. John ripped off the headphones when he saw their guest.

"I don't know how this is happening, John," Brendan said, "but he has come to take me out of here. You can come too." John saw the open door and even though he had missed the suddenness of the angel's appearance, he believed Brendan's explanation. John shook his head.

"No, Father. You are an innocent man, but the right thing for me is to stay and be punished for what I have done."

The angel looked at John: "You are to come too if you will. But I make no promise that you will suffer less by leaving this place."

"Father?" John looked to Brendan.

"Moses was a murderer, son. But God had other plans and Moses never faced Egyptian justice. I believe you should come. Look at my clothes."

John saw that Brendan was not wearing his jumpsuit. Then he looked at his own clothing. The fact that he too was dressed in slacks and a shirt did not strike him as strongly as the discovery of shoes on his feet.

"I haven't worn shoes for over two months! I'll come with you, but what about Jimmy?"

"He will not come," the angel said, "Follow me." John walked out of the cell and went to the door of Jimmy's. Jimmy sat on the edge of his bed.

"Jimmy," John said softly, then louder. "Jimmy!" Jimmy casually looked up in John's direction and saw nothing. He looked away. Brendan took John by the shoulder.

"We have to go," said the stranger. Brendan and John followed him down the hallway past cell after cell, each filled with other men awaiting trial. No one seemed to notice their passing.

"Byrnes here," said the prosecuting attorney, "What's the trouble."

"I'm at the jail." Gonzales was nearly panicked. "These idiots here have not only got Anderson and Daniels in cells right next to each other, but I'm told they have put Brendan Shea into the same cell as John Daniels. He's been there for over two days. I thought we knew better than that!"

"I thought we did too. Stay on the line while I get Cramer on with us." Byrnes was fuming as she waited to get the jail supervisor to the phone. Never, never are co-defendants housed together before trial. On that issue prosecutors and defense attorneys agreed. Prosecutors didn't need defendants cooking their stories together. Defense lawyers are generally wary that something will be said and overheard by the wrong person or that somehow later plea negotiations would be compromised.

At the end of the cell block the angel swung open the barred door easily. The three passed a jailer leading another prisoner in the same hallway. Another jailer soon followed on the run, but he too passed them without notice and entered the cell block from which they just escaped. The double set of electronically controlled exits immediately yielded to the angel's touch and they passed out into a visiting area. There Brendan saw his attorney Gonzales on a pay phone. Gonzales was shouting and looking straight at Brendan, seeing nothing.

"Keep your shirt on Henry," said prosecutor Byrnes, trying to calm Gonzales down. "Cramer was sure they were in different areas but he has a man checking on it right now." Then Cramer came on the line with Byrnes and Gonzales.

"They're gone, Miriam," said Cramer. "Not gone. I mean, they have to be here somewhere, but it seems they were moved a day or so ago. Now Shea and Daniels are not where they are supposed to be. Anderson is still in his cell."

Brendan, John and the angel had not cleared the front door when the alarms went off and every door automatically locked. As the angel led them out, dispatchers were alerting every patrol in the area to converge on the jail. Brendan blinked in the bright sunlight, then he heard the sirens, lots of them, he thought.

"Hurry!" demanded the angel, now walking faster toward the street. They reached the crosswalk. The sirens grew nearer. Brendan saw the flashing lights converging from three directions.

"This is the county jail on our right," said Joe, gesturing out the passenger side window. "There's a municipal garage somewhere around here. Maybe that . . . ." He was interrupted as the car braked suddenly. Father Bertoldi's heart was beating like a rabbit's. He had just managed to stop before hitting a giant of a man who stepped off the curb and faced the car with hand outstretched. Both were still looking at the man when the rear passenger door was flung open and two men jumped into the back seat.

"I think you better drive," Brendan said. Father Bertoldi looked in the rear view mirror at the red-haired man in the rear seat. Then he turned around just to be certain.

"Holiness, this is a surprise," Bertoldi said. He checked ahead and saw that the angel was gone. Then he pressed on the gas.

Chapter Ten

"Mr. President, I wish I could tell you where he has gone, but I cannot even guess what help has been given him," answered the Cardinal. "My sources report nothing of his movements."

"You still do not understand, Scorfazza," said Wolfe accusingly. "Let me explain the gravity of what has happened here. I have known—known for years—that when my time came, there would immediately arise a great challenge to my rule. I did not know what form that challenge would take, but I knew much depended upon defeating that challenge."

"But he is nothing. No one will . . . ." Scorfazza was abruptly cut off as Wolfe continued.

"Then I saw the photo of Brendan Shea in Lindsay's file before your elections. And I knew then that your Eight would choose him. Nothing your idiot Cardinal Reagan said or did was going to have any effect on the outcome."

"Yes, Mr. President. But as you are aware, we were fully prepared and Brendan Shea was arrested even before he could announce himself at the balcony in St. Peter's Square."

"We had him, Scorfazza. Now the most dangerous man on earth has escaped and I expect you to learn where he is to be found."

"I delivered him to you less than 24 hours after his election. It was not my people who let him escape without a trace," said Scorfazza.

"Undoubtedly aided by members of your church whom you seem unable to control," shouted Wolfe accusingly, his face twisted with a hatred never seen on the public man. "Here is what you are going to do. You will provide information on every last Catholic known to be in sympathy with Shea." Wolfe was angry and Scorfazza knew that any further defense of his actions would be useless. Scorfazza held little hope that any thorough list of religious thought criminals could be compiled, but he had long been preparing his own enemies list and would use that as a start. He made only one suggestion.

"Mr. President, we might more easily locate Shea if we did not make it too difficult for him to contact some of his supporters." Wolfe turned to listen to the Cardinal. "I suggest we take no steps against Cardinal Lindsay. Lindsay is his friend and with other courses closed he will have to turn directly to him. When he does, we will be watching."

"Yes, that will be good. Let's do the same with your Cardinal Chiavetta here in Rome. You must make certain that we have trustworthy people alongside those two men. I will see to the electronic surveillance. Thank you, Holy Father," Wolfe said as he rose to let Scorfazza know the interview was at an end. He made use of Scorfazza's newly appropriated papal title only when he knew the Cardinal would be engaged in the unholiest of activities. Scorfazza was walking to the door when Wolfe added: "We will have many opportunities to discuss your progress in finding Brendan Shea. For the present I will be keeping my headquarters here in Rome."

Scorfazza was not pleased to have Wolfe so near, but he had already experienced the complete futility in opposing anything Wolfe commanded. At least he and Wolfe were agreed that the followers of Shea should be suppressed. "Troublers of the Church," he had called them in his first major address after his crowning as pope in Rome.

✥   ✥   ✥

"Wolfe may think Brendan Shea is a danger, but it is Chiavetta who is the thorn in my side and now I cannot even remove him as planned," Scorfazza told Michael Bern, an American priest doing his graduate studies in Rome. Father Bern's academic work had been on hold since Scorfazza enlisted him as an aide after the elections. The lean young priest was prematurely balding and what hair remained was graying fast. He had come to Scorfazza's attention as a great supporter of the new ideas, but his physical appearance and his continuous habit of wearing his black cassock and roman collar (when so many of the newer men spent their off-duty hours in sport shirts and shorts) lent Bern a patina of orthodoxy. With Bern as a personal aide, Scorfazza felt more like a real "Holy Father." Sometimes the Cardinal could almost forget how his master Wolfe enjoyed mocking the new "pope."

Bern was the man Scorfazza assigned to track Chiavetta's activities and no one knew better than Bern how much his boss despised the old Cardinal. Since the elections, Chiavetta had taken up a new vocation in denouncing Scorfazza as "anti-pope" and trumpeting the leadership of Brendan Shea.

"You will be getting to know the Cardinal better," Scorfazza told Father Bern, "once we have placed you into Chiavetta's office." Before the arrangements could be made, however, the old Cardinal suffered a series of strokes that silenced his voice and left him paralyzed and seemingly near death.

Scorfazza wasted no time in seizing the opportunity to display an uncharacteristic and public graciousness to his now toothless enemy and made a show of permitting Chiavetta a comfortable but isolated retirement. Bagnozzi had remained as secretary to the ailing Cardinal. Meanwhile Scorfazza limited Michael Bern's time with the Cardinal to weekly visits sufficient to assure Scorfazza that the Cardinal would not trouble him again.

In his first official papal act, Scorfazza, with the approval of the bishops, had authorized the ordination of thousands of women as priestesses. Most were now presiding over the many priestless parishes that had already employed them as parish "administrators." Scorfazza himself ordained the first hundred, immediately consecrating them as bishops. Then he elevated seven to the Cardinalate, in symbolic replacement of the seven who had voted for Shea.

Spiritual retreats were hastily organized for every male priest and bishop. Each underwent a crash course on the history and relationship of Christianity and fascism. Reeducation in an earthier spirituality was ordered. The new emphasis replaced such outdated concepts as sin and redemption.

The creation-centered faction had made great strides during the twilight years of Clement's reign but had not sufficient time to groom the next generation of teachers. The demand for instructors was worldwide, and so was the shortage. A central database was created to meet the voracious appetite for teachers. From the United States came Native-American and Eskimo shamans. Druids from the British Isles, African witchdoctors and Haitian voodoo practitioners jetted everywhere as guest lecturers. Under the revised canon law no Catholic seminary could function without one witch on the faculty. One prestigious school hired an entire coven and granted them immediate tenure as part of the contract.

Michael Bern had idolized Cardinal Scorfazza and was honored to be able to work closely with him. He approved of the rapid changes being pressed upon the church, but he felt an increasing unease during his service at the Vatican. In the beginning he saw the takeover by new and strange people as a bright sign of health in the Church. He saw himself as part of the problem: too many straight male priests with no idea of life outside the walls. Priests like me, he thought.

Scorfazza had boasted that he would make the Vatican as diverse as the world itself. He liked to say that was the meaning of the term "Catholic." As far as Bern could tell, this chiefly meant the addition of a number of sturdy women and effeminate young men to populate the corridors of the Vatican. Scorfazza established a rotating board of theologians as a ruling church council, but manipulated its makeup to insure his own control. Scorfazza saw to it that an ample number of Protestants, as well as eastern religionists were well represented on the council and decreed that at least two children, a boy and a girl would also be voting members. Then there was the new prefect of the Congregation for the Doctrine of the Faith. Short and round, the bull-necked Mary Ellen Cardinal Eckhardt was called "Eminence" to her face, but the young men referred to the former nun with the butch haircut as "Torqemada."

Michael Bern had no problem with the females now filling jobs in the Roman curia. He easily grew accustomed to fellow priests with earrings and pierced cheeks. Even so, he felt a growing unquiet. He gave no label to the unease, and for a time he continued to dismiss from his mind what he had not yet named; but the uncleanness, the meanness all about him only grew with time. It seemed the glorious and high minded principles that had attracted him to the new church leadership only made more conspicuous the widening gap between those principles and the vulgarity and uncharity of the men and women Scorfazza continued to bring to his inner circle.

If he had stayed more by Scorfazza's side Bern might have been reconciled with the breach between ideals and actions, but Bern was living in two worlds.

Scorfazza had taken the name John to suggest identification with the last pope of that name. The cause of Pope John XXIII for sainthood had been moving ahead quickly when one day Michael Bern was making his regular report to the "Holy Father." Scorfazza was in high spirits, but seemed distracted as Bern spoke. The anti-pope had picked up a newspaper and started to put on his reading glasses when he stopped and buzzed his secretary.

"Is Cardinal Eckhardt in today?" Her Eminence was, and soon joined them. "Have you seen this?" Scorfazza asked as he handed the article to the former nun. She began to scan it silently when he added, "Out loud, Eminence. Please. The highlighted part if you would." She began.

"The new Pope John is devoted to the memory of his predecessor John XXIII. Our present Holy Father is far too humble to see the truth, but it is he who brought the Second Vatican Counsel to full flower and glory, and he who deserves to be known as "good Pope John."

At the words "good Pope John," Bern snorted, a sound halfway between laughter and disgust that he quickly stifled with alarm. Fortunately for Bern, Cardinal Eckhardt's own obsequious squeal of agreement effectively masked the priest's outburst. Scorfazza became positively joyous as he blushed with unmitigated pleasure. Michael smiled and thought to himself: how much more he had respected the lady Cardinal in the old days when the little nun gave no quarter to any man. Then he frowned as something inside turned that same mirror on himself.

Bern had been keeping his weekly visits to Chiavetta's side now for several months. There was no pretense made as to the purpose of his visits. He was to provide an early warning should Chiavetta threaten to rise from his bed once again to bedevil the people of God. During those visits Bern discovered that Father Bagnozzi was a scholar like himself and—his outdated ideas notwithstanding—a kind and congenial host.

Each time Bern drove to Chiavetta's bedside, he felt an ironic sadness that the man Bern served, the man who championed the new ideas, possessed not even a hint of what would have been called holiness in an earlier day. Scorfazza was a liar, thought Bern. His only loyalty was to himself; and, in some limited way, to the man Wolfe, the only person whom

Scorfazza feared. Bern could not forget the sight of his "pope" trembling after an interview with the president.

Bern found himself increasingly disturbed by the contrast between the Byzantine scheming of the new Vatican and the simple-hearted cheer of the sickroom of his ostensible enemy, Cardinal Chiavetta. The Cardinal had insisted that Bern and Bagnozzi join him for meals whenever Bern would visit. Bern had continued to report Chiavetta's total physical and mental incapacity. In fact, he had quickly discerned that the Cardinal's mind was unaffected by his illness. Now that Cardinal Chiavetta was speaking intelligibly, Bern knew he should upgrade his reporting, but he had not done so. Had he thought about it, Bern might have admitted and corrected his lapse, but Bern had begun to enjoy getting away from Rome. It would simply not occur to him to change his relationship with the Cardinal with whom he so disagreed, or thought he disagreed.

The early spring air was chilly that morning when Bern set out for his weekly visit to the Cardinal, but the sun was up and would soon warm the Italian countryside. Something made him think of his favorite professor in the seminary. It had been the ridicule of that popular priest that had led to his abandonment of his daily prayers in the seminary. He reflected how his studies began to substitute for devotions; and how his pride of accomplishment took the place of humility. He laughed out loud, but sadly, as he thought how little pride he now felt at his new life.

Last evening he had come in late and stopped to look up at the same Roman sky that Brendan Shea had prayed beneath on the night before his election. But where Shea had seen the hand of God, Bern was struck cold by the desolation he felt. He had always loved the small things; a rioting spring breaking out of a hillside, a baby's smile; even a tiny frog hopping along a damp path in the woods. Now such beauties were overshadowed by a world turned ugly. As a man whose faith had slowly moved from God to the world, Bern felt betrayed. This is despair, he told himself, curious that he could stand outside himself and see it, yet with no diminution of the emptiness.

Bern parked where the circle drive came nearest the house. Most days he would step lightly up the stone walkway, free for a few hours from the gray vocation his life had become. Today his personal cloud was thicker and Bern's step was slow as he walked up and rang the bell.

"Father Bern, come in," said Bagnozzi as he opened the double doors. "Cardinal Chiavetta is anxious to see you."

"Hello, Joseph," he answered dully.

Father Bagnozzi frowned to see Bern troubled and weighed down. Normally the priest was lighthearted and affable during his visits and Bagnozzi had become accustomed to the pleasantness surrounding these weekly calls. It was easy for him to forget that Father Bern was the emissary of a man whose every move, every decision, seemed calculated to destroy whatever faith remained on the earth. As he took Bern's coat he recalled the Cardinal's questioning about whether Bern were expected today. He realized that the old man had seemed to anticipate this dark change in Father Bern.

Michael Bern went straight to the solarium where the Cardinal spent most of his days through the winter. Bagnozzi followed, but only as far as the door of the large bright room and waited to see what would happen. Bern did not greet Chiavetta but sat in front of him on a stool.

"Are you ready to come back, son?" the old man asked him.

Michael Bern sobbed and tried to speak. "I can't . . . I can't go back."

"Certainly you can go back. Seventy times seven times can you go back, if you will. You must choose."

"I have chosen, Eminence," he said, straightening himself. "Will you hear my confession? I put myself in your will as the will of Christ," he finally said with resolve. Bagnozzi backed from the doorway to leave them alone. When Father Bern had finished he fell silent again and stayed so for several minutes.

"You are thinking how good it is to come back, Father?" the elder man remarked, shaking the priest from his daydream.

"I was thinking that the Holy Spirit is too good to bear. It is overwhelming to be given my life back after having traveled so far away from the God of my youth. But to be released from the stench in Rome at the very same time is more blessing than I can hold at once. Dreading the pains of hell may not be the purest motive for salvation, but when you've had a taste of it, it does drive one in the other direction." Bern was smiling now. "That's what I meant when I said I couldn't go back."

The smile disappeared when the Cardinal next spoke. "But you must go back. The Holy Father needs you in Rome."

 Chapter Eleven

"Have you heard if Father Bagnozzi will join us this evening?" asked Brendan Shea.

"Yes, but he is only now arriving in the city, Father" said John.

Brendan had been in exile and hiding in the city for more than two years. Compared to Rome, and the rest of the world, Jerusalem had been a relatively hospitable place for the man who was both head of the outlawed church and a fugitive from American justice.

When the dust settled from Brendan's election, arrest and escape, the split in the Catholic Church was worse than even the eight Cardinals had feared. In a free world, Brendan might have been followed by a third of the Catholic Church at the time of his election. But under the growing power of Mason Wolfe the world was far from free, and fear had so seized the Body of Christ that not one soul in ten could be counted as remaining in unity with Pope Brendan and the Church he led.

Most considered that Scorfazza, allied with Wolfe and now presiding over the larger body of Catholics, had won. Even so, a hundred million faithful still followed Brendan and opposed the new political and religious order. Open opposition to Wolfe had been ruthlessly crushed. Already he had orchestrated the arrest of a million people in the United States, all accused of being terrorists. Confined to re-education camps, they worked as slave labor. More than five million Christians were interned worldwide. Most of those were Catholics but many were not.

The great apostasy, or falling away from the faith that old Bishop Shopra had diagnosed, was a world-wide phenomenon. As it took hold, Brendan sought out Christians everywhere. He sent messages to the traditionalist Catholic groups that had separated themselves from the Pope years before. "We must be one. Come back," he told them.

The traditionalists had been badly splintered for years. Many had claimed loyalty to Clement XV, but would not obey him. Others claimed there was no pope at all and a dozen tiny sects claimed their own elected leader as pope. The only thing the traditionalists could agree on was that the Church must return to the old Latin Mass.

Indeed, there came a widespread surge of interest in the older, pre-Vatican II ways. Brendan knew his flock would follow if he were to abolish the vernacular language in the Mass and prescribe Latin only, but he would make no such order. Brendan did bring an abrupt end to what some had called the "liturgical fidget," those free and casual innovations of the most sacred ritual of the Church. But Brendan Shea was steadfast in leaving Catholics free when that freedom did not interfere with the essential oneness of the faith.

He reminded the faithful that unity means unity of doctrine, what Catholics profess publicly; and unity means unity of government, by which all submit to one leadership, as instituted by Christ Himself. And finally, Brendan had written, unity means unity of worship, as manifested by the same sacrifice and in the reception of the same sacraments. Regarding ceremonial forms, he had continued, both the ancient rites and the modern vernacular forms are approved, for these do not hinder our essential unity of worship.

Most of the traditionalists did come back; some eagerly and others warily. Those that stayed away became increasingly isolated and eccentric in their doctrinal interpretation. More and more they seemed a bizarre parody of Protestantism, holding fiercely to some trusted anchor, be it the Baltimore Catechism or the teachings of a particular pope or council, now centuries in the grave.

The tumult among Catholics came at the same time as an explosion in the number of Protestant sects. Tiny cells of leaderless Christians met quietly in homes and many began to look to Brendan Shea's Church as the only open, large-scale opposition to Mason Wolfe's leadership. As for those Catholic faithful who had stayed with Brendan, Wolfe would not forever tolerate the continued freedom and existence of those 100 million plus rebels.

Father Bagnozzi arrived long after dark with messages from Cardinal Chiavetta in Rome. Monsignor Tom Bertoldi, now serving as Brendan's secretary, sat in the meeting, as did John Daniels. Visitors had long been accustomed to John's constant presence with the young pope.

"Tell me first how is Cardinal Chiavetta's health?" Brendan asked.

"He is doing very well except for some weakness on one side. He cannot write, but his mind is perfect and in constant motion. Of course only a few are aware of his recovery at all."

"Do we still have our source inside the Vatican?" Brendan asked, unwilling to speak more openly of Michael Bern's role as double agent in Rome. Bern's job was the same as it had been from the beginning. In addition to the various projects that Scorfazza assigned to him, Bern still made his weekly visits to Chiavetta.

"Yes. And I have word of a new liturgical rite that is soon to be promulgated."

"More of the same watering down and mother earth sort of thing?"

"They have been very secretive about the changes," said Bagnozzi, "For months, Scorfazza has been meeting with a core of priests. Now we know they have developed the new rite . . . ."

"A new mass?" Brendan interrupted.

". . . with Mason Wolfe," finished Bagnozzi.

"Wolfe," repeated the Pope, as if it were not even a surprise.

"Recently, Eckhardt has been bringing in large numbers of priests from all over. She is conducting training sessions on the new ritual."

"Is it true they call her Torquemada? Rather an unfair comparison, don't you think?" Brendan asked.

"Well if your holiness knew the sister better . . . ."

"Unfair to Tomas de Torquemada, I mean." Bertoldi and John showed smiles, but Bagnozzi was unaccustomed to Brendan's habit of making a jest at the most serious of moments. "What else can you tell me about it?"

"While the whole thing has been so secret that no one outside Scorfazza's circle and the newly-trained priests are even aware of its existence, we expect an announcement sometime soon. Every indication we have, Holiness, is that we may be seeing the end of the Mass in Scorfazza's church, that is, if you can call what they are doing these days 'Mass.'"

It would be late into the night when Father Bagnozzi concluded his briefing. Brendan was most encouraged by his report on the still new monastic movement, which had been growing like a summer wildfire. A layman of Brendan's acquaintance, Joe Dupre, had set it in motion just three years before.

After Brendan's escape from jail, Dupre had hidden both Brendan and John Daniels in his home east of Kansas City while Father Bertoldi made arrangements for them to leave the country. For that week, the attorney and the mass murderer attended daily morning mass celebrated by the pope. Then Dupre would go to his office in the city, only to hurry home later to spend the evening in talk with John and Brendan.

Joe loved God and he loved the Church, but he was often distressed at his failures with sin and the seeming dryness of his spiritual life. Every prayer had been for the grace to make his life and soul pleasing to God and Joe always felt something was missing. Then Brendan and John came. Joe could not understand how John could be so joyful, even exuberant, and yet peaceful at the same time. When he spoke of it to Brendan, he was reminded that few men had sunk so low as John, and even fewer had been forgiven so much. The Lord carries him, Brendan had explained.

"You wish he still carried you, Joseph?" Brendan had asked. "He will not carry you again, but he will take you so completely into His life that you will walk on your own. You have to pray."

When Brendan finally left, Joseph did pray. The more that he prayed the more time he spent away from his law practice, promoting the cause of Brendan Shea and his shrunken Church. It was later that year that Joe Dupre was arrested as he left Sunday Mass at one of the few Kansas City churches still loyal to Brendan Shea.

Joseph Dupre, or Brother Joe, as he came to be called, was one of the first detainees in the central regional detention camp. Eventually there were 300,000 detainees in the camp, nearly all followers of Brendan Shea. In the beginning it was Brother Joe and two men, but in less than three years the *Prisoners of Christ* had grown to more than a million men and women, most of whom were literal prisoners in the network of concentration camps that now dotted the earth.

The *Prisoners* each took a monk's vows of chastity, poverty and obedience, obedience to his immediate superior and to Pope Brendan. The monastic rules of life were very similar to those followed for over a thousand years, but with a unique division of labor between the great majority of members who were in fact incarcerated and those members who lived outside the camps. At every moment, twenty-fours hours a day, more than 100,000 souls offered up the incense of prayers for a single intention: for the conversion of the billions now in the worldwide stranglehold of Mason Wolfe. Judging from the accelerating stream of persons into the camps, the *Prisoners* on the outside enjoyed the benefits of that supernatural assist, for not since Pentecost had so few successfully evangelized so many of their neighbors. Even as one of their number was arrested and sent to a camp, three new converts would rise in his place.

"Many things of God are a mystery," observed Brendan, "but the *Prisoners of Christ*—in light of history—now seem an obvious development. Besides his love for God, what causes a man to renounce the world? Times of great evil and greed? Add persecution and separation from home and possessions, separation from work and family. Throw in a well-founded belief that Christ's coming may be near."

"Very much like the first centuries of the Church," said Bertoldi.

"Yes, and although there was some movement toward communal property at the time, nothing like what we would call a Christian monastic order would exist until about 300 A.D. The difference now is that instead of fleeing persecution and a faithless world, our monks stay and thrive on the persecution. Then when Wolfe gets around to arresting them, they're gathered up and situated together in one place in the desert. Our brother Joe had been long in the preparing and I am sure he had not imagined where his visit to the jail that day would lead."

"Nor did any of us," said Bagnozzi.

"I can understand Wolfe and Scorfazza not anticipating the rise of the order of *Prisoners*, for we did not foresee its coming either," said Bertoldi, "but thinking they could quash the movement by splitting up Joe's original group into a dozen other camps was unbelievable blindness on their part. The Holy Spirit has had a field day and all the while Wolfe is acting as unwitting host for the increase."

"How long can he allow us to gain at his expense?" asked Bagnozzi.

"Wolfe is not finished with us. He waits to see who are his enemies. And it has taken time for him to consolidate his power," Brendan said. "It's safe to say that most countries not directly controlled by him will follow his lead, either by choice or by coercion."

"We have been fortunate that Israel has remained independent and turned a blind eye to Christians here," offered Bertoldi. "If Wolfe knew you were here, he would not be so lenient about the suppression of the Church here in Jerusalem."

"He knows. He is waiting for a day when the city belongs to him alone. But for now he honors his agreement with the Israeli government. That will change," Brendan said. "I think I will take advantage of our freedom tomorrow."

It was one of those rare occasions when Brendan got away from the press of his work. Even rarer were his opportunities to visit the holy sites of Jerusalem. That Sabbath afternoon, Brendan left his headquarters in an Arab neighborhood north of the ancient walled city. On foot and alone, he was dressed as an ordinary Jerusalemite, his red hair covered with a cap. It was just a ten minute walk to St. Stephen's Gate from the small monastery where he made his home. As Brendan neared the northeast corner of the old walled city, the Mount of Olives was to his left. From that distance he could see the Garden of Gethsemani where Jesus prayed in anguish before his arrest on that night so many years before. At that place Brendan's forebears, the apostles, abandoned their Master and ran for their lives.

Brendan thought uneasily about his own flight from danger and wondered about his underground governance of the Church. He had spent a thousand nights in anguished prayer for his suffering Church. Uncertainty, dread and guilt marked his lowest times. Why had he continued to live in relative safety while so many of his brothers and sisters lived in fear, or chains, or both? There had been some who counseled him to return to Rome. That was his place. In Rome he might have confronted Scorfazza directly. Bold heroics appealed to Brendan superficially, but whenever he asked, his prayers brought him no peace about that course of action.

He had come to accept that his task was first to reorganize the Church during her hardship and imprisonment; and next, to harden the Body of Christ for suffering and death and glory to come. Brendan sensed that events had quickened and that his own quiet time might be ending.

As Brendan neared the walls, he could make out the old Jewish cemetery. It was the oldest cemetery still in use in the world and consumed much of the western side of the Mount of Olives. An ancient tradition held that at the coming of the messiah the dead would be raised and follow him into Jerusalem through the Mercy Gate, opposite the Mount of Olives. Brendan reflected that until a few months before, the resurrected would have had to walk through the solid rock and mortar of the walled-over gate. The Moslems, harboring old memories of crusader conquests, had a legend that the Christian king who would next rule the city would also pass through the same gate. Indeed, that is why it was so carefully walled over centuries ago.

But now the way that Jesus had passed on Palm Sunday had been reopened. The gate had been heavily damaged during the earthquake that destroyed the Dome of the Rock and the repair had provided the occasion to reopen it. Now the Jews would be ready for the coming of the messiah.

Since its re-dedication, the Mercy Gate had become the favored path for pilgrims and worshippers making their way to the magnificent new temple that now dominated the skyline of Old Jerusalem. Even the resplendent Moslem Dome of the Rock, yet to be rebuilt, would not command attention like the creamy white marble mountain that was the new Jewish temple. Brendan could easily see the temple from his home in the newer part of the city, but now he was in the shadow of the weathered brown city walls built by the great Ottoman Sultan, Suleiman the Magnificent. To Brendan, the massive honey-colored stone walls appeared as a mere fence before the bright towering facade of the temple.

Brendan was not going to the temple and so entered the Old City north of the Mercy Gate at the entrance known as St. Stephen's or the Lion's gate, with its sculpted lions in stone relief on either side of the opening. Outside that gate, two thousand years before, a Jew named Saul of Tarsus stood holding the coats of angry men as they stoned the first Christian martyr. Brendan passed inside and went straight ahead toward the west, keeping the temple on his left.

It had been a long while since Brendan had felt it necessary to remain in constant hiding. Even though he allowed himself a day's freedom on occasion, he was always mindful that he was still a fugitive who might be arrested at any time. He was watchful inside the old city, especially near the temple where Israeli troops and police were always a strong presence. The Moslem Dome of the Rock had not been rebuilt and the peace of Jerusalem, wrought three and a half years before by Mason Wolfe, had begun to fray at the edges. The old animosities between Moslem and Jew were becoming more open. Brendan was surprised to find very little security in place when he came through the gate that day.

On his right he passed near the Church of St. Anne, site of the birth of Mary the mother of Jesus. Nearby is the pool of Bethesda, where Jesus healed a lame man. Brendan kept on another few hundred yards until he came to the area of the Antonia Fortress, the location of Pontius Pilate's judgment hall. Here Brendan finally stopped. Here was the place where Jesus was condemned to death and given his cross to carry: the *Via Dolorosa*, the Way of Sorrows; the Way of the Cross.

The day before, on Friday, he might have joined the weekly Franciscan procession, but today Brendan would make his pilgrimage through the narrow street alone. Brendan imagined he could still hear the 2000 year old dialogue still echoing in that ancient place:

"What shall I do, then, with Jesus who is called Christ?" Pilate asked. They all answered, "Crucify him!"

"Why? What crime has he committed?" asked Pilate. But they shouted all the louder, "Crucify him!" So Pilate took water and washed his hands saying,

"I am innocent of this man's blood." Then they answered back.

"Let his blood be on us and on our children!"

Brendan walked to the next station, stopping to pray. And so he stopped at each station as he made his way past the traditional sites: the place where Jesus first fell under the weight of the cross, the place his grieving mother met her son and where Simon of Cyrene was drafted to carry the cross. Brendan slowly worked his way through the Moslem quarter of the old city.

He started uphill, stopping where the woman stepped out from the crowd to wipe the face of Jesus, where Jesus fell again, and where Jesus told the women of Jerusalem not to weep for him, but for themselves and their children. Finally, Brendan came through the courtyard and church of an Ethiopian monastery to enter the Church of the Holy Sepulcher. On that site, now occupied by the decrepit, ancient crusader church, the Romans had crucified his Lord. Here they had laid the tortured body of Jesus in his mother's arms and then sealed him in the rock tomb.

Brendan was overwhelmed by the thought of his own sinfulness as he prayed at the Holy Sepulcher. Here, his Lord had paid the full measure for all mankind. Brendan stayed long and prayed about his Church. When he finished, Brendan thought absently that he ought not have knelt so long and so publicly. But none of that seemed to matter now, for in that hour the Spirit had lifted him. He knew his time of waiting, his time of questioning, was over.

By the time Brendan walked back outdoors, the late afternoon sunlight had left most of the city in shadow, but the fading rays had transformed the temple to the east into purest gold. It was time to get home and Brendan began to retrace his steps toward the temple and the Lion's Gate. At this hour tourists were not lingering and pedestrians all seemed intent on getting somewhere before dusk. Not likely, Brendan thought, that anyone would pay him any attention during the walk home.

Since his escape from the jail in Kansas City, Brendan had so frequently caught glances of recognition from other people, that he no longer anticipated his immediate capture each time someone stared at him for too long. The contrary was true, for Brendan's experience with being recognized had been more a blessing than a curse. The first time it had happened was as he was about to board his flight out of the United States. The customs agent was questioning Brendan too closely for comfort when the agent's supervisor approached and waved Brendan on. Brendan was already the most wanted man on earth and was disguised as much as practicable. So he was shocked when the supervisor handed him his bag and said in a low voice: "Please go on, Holy Father." Brendan nodded and passed through. Today he had caught his share of glances, but as usual, no one had run to fetch the police.

✠ ✠ ✠

"Can you come to the atrium," the young monk said to John. "These fellows asked to see John Daniels. Is your last name Daniels?" John nodded. "The men also said they need to see the pope." That information—that Brendan Shea was a guest of the monastery—was not known by any monk other than the abbot. Now two strangers were calling for the accused killers. John wished that the Holy Father had not gone out for the day.

"Thank you, Brother David, I'll be right up."

John walked slowly into the entryway where both visitors stood. One was a shorter, powerfully built man. John thought he would be in his thirties. Rough, and wild looking, John thought. Put him on the banks of the Jordan river, wearing a hair shirt, and there would be a picture of John the Baptist. The taller man was older, with graying hair. The eyes, John noticed, were deep and seemed far older than the dignified face that framed them. It was the deep-eyed one that spoke first.

"You are John Daniels, correct?"

"Yes." He had not meant to make such an admission, but now he made no effort to hide his identity.

"You are wanted for murder in the United States. You live here with the bishop of Rome, Brendan Shea, and with his secretary, Monsignor Thomas Bertoldi. You also have a guest here from Rome, a Father Bagnozzi."

"Our time is short," the younger man urged, "You must all leave with us right away."

"Why should anyone come with you? I don't even know who you are!"

"This is not the time for much talk. You will have to trust that we are not enemies. Mason Wolfe knows you are here. His people will be here today to arrest you." John did not know what to do, but it seemed that he and the others had no secrets from these men, except that the strangers did not seem to realize that Brendan was not at home.

"Brendan Shea is not here today," John said, not being able to think of anything else to say. Each of the two looked at the other. The wild looking one appeared uneasy with that information. Finally, John decided to get some help. "Let's go to our rooms and see Monsignor Bertoldi," continued John. The men repeated their story for Bertoldi and Bagnozzi. The two men, who gave no name, did not convince Father Bagnozzi. He was more accustomed to life in Rome where espionage had become a way of life, and a man—even a man of God—brought a certain measure of distrust to any unfamiliar situation.

"Then you must at least tell me who you are," insisted Bertoldi.

"We will do so, but not until we meet with Brendan Shea."

Bertoldi was especially suspicious of the strangers' insistence upon telling their full tale only in the presence of Brendan Shea. He remained unconvinced, but finally acquiesced, knowing that they and Brendan could be as easily betrayed here at the monastery as on the outside. Despite the strangers' urging that they and Brendan Shea were in great danger, Father Bagnozzi was relieved that they did not have to decide whether to lead the strangers to Brendan, for they did not know where Brendan had gone.

"We'll go with you," said Bertoldi and in thirty minutes they were gone, together with all the records and papers of the Church in exile.

Brendan had reached the area of the temple and was headed back toward the Lion's gate. Then he heard shouts coming near from behind him. Seconds later five or six young men rushed past him and kept running toward the temple. Several of them had guns and none paid him any attention. Before they reached the mount there came more shouting from above and then some popping sounds. Gunfire, thought Brendan. He debated whether he should go forward in the shadow of the temple or make some other way out of the old city. Brendan went ahead.

Still some distance away from the Lion's Gate, he stopped as a stream of men in gray uniforms suddenly came through the gate. This was clearly a military force of some kind, although the uniforms were not those of the familiar Israeli army. Brendan immediately turned left, to the north, to make for Herod's Gate and hoped he would not find more troops in that direction.

Brendan had been walking north for only a minute when he heard footsteps behind him. When he glanced back he saw two men silhouetted against the sunset, but they did not appear to be soldiers. He walked on for half a block but the feet gained on him. He was about to turn and confront them when one spoke.

"Brendan Shea?"

"Who are you?" he asked. He did not particularly like the ragged looks of the two, especially the younger, shorter man.

"You will not get back to the monastery that way," said the taller man. Brendan looked to the north and could see another patrol like the one he had seen at the Lion's gate. "Wolfe's troops are taking over the city. You will be safe only if you come with us."

The sun would soon set. Brendan knew no other way out of the old city. "It is the time," the taller one continued, "ours, and yours."

Brendan looked skyward, as if for a sign. After a few moments he nodded with a sudden assurance. "Alright," he said, letting them take the lead. They walked quickly through the streets of the Moslem Quarter. "Where are we going?" Brendan asked as they stopped at the sound of a patrol vehicle approaching from behind.

"Not far. Just keep walking," said the older of the two. The patrol stopped and two soldiers got out twenty feet behind them.

"Halt!" shouted one soldier.

"Do not stop. Keep walking. They are looking for you, Brendan Shea."

"Halt or we will shoot!" the soldier shouted again, and more insistent. Brendan pulled up short at the click of a weapon's safety being switched off. The two strangers turned as Brendan stopped. Then Brendan saw each soldier raise his automatic weapon and he realized they were going to fire. At the same time he saw the shorter of his companions raise his arm. Brendan felt something like a charge in the air and then there was a great flash, which left Brendan momentarily blinded. His companions took him by the arm and they hurried up the street.

"What happened? Brendan asked.

"They were going to kill us," said the shorter one. "Don't look back now. Keep moving. They are dead." Brendan noticed they were bearing back to the east and parallel to the *Via Dolorosa*, which Brendan had followed on his way into the heart of the old city. Soon they would come to the Church of St. Anne and Pools of Bethesda on their right.

"Here we are," said the younger man. They stopped at a two-story building made of the same honey-colored stone so familiar throughout the city. Brendan followed the two inside and up the stairs to a large upper room where he found John Daniels, Bertoldi and Bagnozzi.

"Holy Father! You are safe!" John had leapt up and embraced Brendan in a rush of relief, relief that his trust in the two strangers had not gone awry. "We didn't know what to do. These men came and said Wolfe's men were coming. They brought us here and said don't go out. That was hours ago."

"You must be hungry," said the older stranger to Brendan, motioning for everyone to sit down at the table. "Mrs. Habash's table is without peer in all the Middle East. We will eat, then talk." John had not realized how hungry he was until the widow Habash began to fill the long table with appetizers: olives, nuts, raisins and salted chick peas, four kinds of pickles made from turnips, beets and onions, as well as cucumbers. Ground lamb patties, fresh greens, and bread spread with olive oil and soft cheese left precious little space on the table for eating. The crowded table notwithstanding, they had no trouble eating and drinking to everyone's satisfaction as they talked about what each had seen that day in the city.

The elder stranger remarked that the Israeli government had good relations with Wolfe, but that was only because he had been Israel's protector since the waning of U.S. military power. For reasons seemingly known only to President Wolfe, Israel had continued to enjoy a measure of freedom and autonomy enjoyed by few other nations. Cordial relations notwithstanding, the Israeli government had not consented to the outrage of this takeover of Israeli soil; an outrage enabled by the Merovingians.

The Merovingians were but a small faction within the civilian Israeli government. Within the military, however, the messianic ultra-religious party had grown large and could be found in the highest places. They took their name from the line of French kings whom Wolfe claimed as his ancestors and whom they believed were Jews of the lineage of King David. Now with the help of Merovingian treason, Mason Wolfe controlled the Old City while the Israeli army sat on the sidelines.

"The troops we escaped today," explained the elder stranger, "were members of Mason Wolfe's Global Defense Alliance, now called by its initials, the GDA." With very little opposition, the GDA has taken over the area of the temple only blocks from where we now sit. They are still securing the area within the old city walls, but they failed in one of their key objectives . . . ."

"To arrest me?" questioned Brendan. The two strangers nodded. "I am indebted. We are indebted to you for our freedom and lives and would seem to be safe at the moment. I pray our brothers at the monastery were not harmed. You have surely proven faithful with our trust, gentlemen, but I hope you know better than I the reason we are here." Brendan waited for a response, but it was Bagnozzi who spoke to Brendan.

"Excuse me, Holy Father, but do you speak Italian?"

"Not much," Brendan replied, puzzled at the question.

"Then how is it you understand the perfect Italian he is speaking?" Bagnozzi asked, "And why do you then answer them in English?"

"Because they are speaking English." Both men looked back at the two strangers.

"Actually, we have been speaking Hebrew," the shorter stranger interjected, "You only hear us in your native tongue."

Brendan stood and fixed his gaze on the rough-looking stranger. "Who are you?"

"My name is Elijah."

"The prophet?" Brendan asked pointedly. John had leaned back on two legs of his stool, his hands massaging an overfull stomach, when he very nearly lost his balance hearing Brendan's unexpected question. The man nodded affirmatively and turned to his older companion.

"And this is Enoch." Father Bagnozzi was still trying to put together the part about Elijah the prophet, when something from his memory clicked on at the reference to Enoch.

"Enoch? The *Book of Enoch*, Enoch?" the Italian asked, turning to the gray headed one. The elder man thought a moment about the reference and answered Bagnozzi.

"I am the man you are speaking of, but I can't claim to have written most of the work you mentioned."

"You will find my co-worker modest to the point of withholding information," said Elijah, "and considering the trials that you will face with us, I want to answer fully your questions. Then we will discuss our task."

"Where have you come from?" asked John. "From heaven? Are you the same men from the Old Testament?"

"No, actually we have never been to heaven; can't say we know any more than you about it. But yes, we are those men from the past, and we are real men, doomed to die, as are other men."

Elijah explained an experience that had been unique to himself and Enoch. When the fiery chariot carried him skyward so many centuries ago, Elijah had left his disciple Elisha to wear the prophetic mantle in Israel. He found himself in the in-between place, called by some, "paradise."

"At first, I thought I had been transported to some beautiful but unpopulated country on earth. In that lush greenness, I was suddenly not hungry, not tired, and completely content; so I sat down in the short grass, as soft as goose feathers. And waited.

"Perhaps 'waiting' is not the word I should use to describe it, do you think, Enoch?" Elijah said as he looked to his old friend. "I mean it hardly seems like waiting when you are so happy that the best thing that can happen is nothing. And that is what happened, at least until Father Enoch came to me. He said he had walked a long time to reach me since the others had first told him of my arrival."

"I would have come to greet you sooner," the elder man said, remembering the long past meeting, "but paradise had grown so much since I arrived, I had no idea how many strides separated us. Not a few, it seemed."

"If it was paradise, then shouldn't it have been filled with people by your time?" John asked.

"Oh, it was!" Elijah said, "All around me, they were, but I did not see them until Enoch came. His greeting was a prayer. 'Father, may he see also?' No sooner did he say it, but then my eyes were opened, and I saw them all, those who had died before my departure."

"Father Abraham, you met him?" questioned Father Bertoldi. "Isaac and Jacob and Moses? King David?"

Elijah smiled, remembering, and nodded his head. "It was as marvelous as you imagine, my friend, almost more than I could bear. Near the end of that time there came the first of those who had actually seen the Holy One of God. I remember the old man Simeon who saw the Redeemer, the Glory of Israel, as an infant. And there were those Persian Kings that found him in a stable. One by one, the dead brought us news that the Messiah was alive and walked the earth, and still, we did not realize who he was."

"Until his father came . . . or his adoptive father he was," said Enoch. "Joseph was the one who told us who He was, but even then it was difficult to understand. You all know that Elijah met the Messiah once before he was crucified?"

"But even now I cannot speak of that," Elijah interrupted. "Still, we did not truly grasp what His coming to Israel meant. Finally, He came to us in paradise: the Lamb of God and King of all Kings; the Son of God. Then we began to understand. He spoke to all the people and said he would lead us to His Father in heaven. We were completely taken with delight," Elijah said, remembering the day.

"You cannot imagine the joy! Before he left, Jesus turned aside to speak to Enoch and myself. He said we had not yet finished our work; that we would not come with the others. I would have been sad if sorrow were not impossible in that place. So He left with them all in His train and we were left alone. Paradise was small again and Enoch and I, its only inhabitants. Meanwhile, nearly two thousand years passed in Israel."

Each man sat silently with his own thoughts for a time; Enoch and Elijah recalling the day; the others trying to imagine the experience. Then Brendan Shea turned to other questions.

"Let me ask you Enoch, you said you didn't write most of the Book of Enoch. Did you write some of it?"

"I have seen the book that has come down to you, and yes, a bit of it is mine. Specifically, there is a prophecy there that was given through me. It pertains to the present time and the judgment that is coming on the earth: 'And behold! He cometh with ten thousands of His holy ones to execute judgment upon all, And to destroy all the ungodly.' There was more, and not all so dire, but that is all I recognize."

"Enoch has left us far more than a vision of apocalypse," added Elijah. "He is the inventor of writing, a fact not generally known and one he would never tell you. You are probably more acquainted with another work by him. We know it as the first five chapters of the book of Genesis."

Enoch then continued the story. "I later learned it was carried safely through the deluge by my great-grandson Noah. Of course, Moses was inspired to use it in his writings."

"How could you even know about the Garden of Eden and other things that you wrote?" John asked.

"It's true that the Man did not witness the creation, but I wrote it exactly as he told it to me."

"Who told it to you?" said Bertoldi.

"The Man, of course," Enoch said, as if everyone knew what he was talking about. His listeners said nothing, seemingly waiting for him to explain himself. "The Man, you call him Adam, was my ancestor and yours. He still lived in my time and I knew him well. Unfortunately, the old man was held in little esteem in those desolate, evil times. For all his days after the expulsion, Adam worshipped the Lord, but he never forgave himself for the filth and rebellion into which his children had descended. He never stopped grieving over his offense against God and I too grieved to see his suffering, especially after our mother Eve died. He remained the gravest of men until his death. When the Son came to paradise, it was Adam He first greeted, and Adam at the head with Him as he led those poor captives to glory. I cried with happiness to see it." Enoch leaned backward and lost himself in a tranquil silence as he contemplated that Good Friday two millennia before.

For a great part of the evening, the two messengers from paradise tried to satisfy the questions of their four astonished guests. Finally Elijah turned the subject to his last mission. "Holy Father," he began as he turned to Brendan Shea. Neither man had used Brendan's title before that moment and John wondered that it sounded strange on the lips of the great prophet. Brendan, fully as much as John and the two priests, was in awe of the two glorious Old Testament saints, but Elijah knew that Brendan Shea stood in the place of Christ on earth and even he and Enoch would be subject to him.

"Holy Father," he repeated, "tomorrow Mason Wolfe will make a triumphal entry into the city. Holding himself out as the son of David, of the tribe of Judah, he will be proclaimed Messiah and King of the Jews. We will be there to meet him."

Chapter Twelve

The Merovingians had done their work overnight and a huge multitude gathered on the east side of the city between the Temple and the Mount of Olives. Brendan stood just outside the Golden Gate. He, Enoch, Elijah and the others all looked to see what was happening near the top of the Mount. At first it was impossible to make out. Then movement. After a time Brendan began to see that the traveling splotch of color was a group of people slowly moving toward the city.

As the movement started down the Mount they could see a central grouping around a man riding a great Arabian stallion. The horse's golden harness glinted in the morning sun. The people scrambled to cut palm branches and hurried to place them in the path of the horseman. Others laid their coats on the path before him.

"He would come like this," Bertoldi said aloud. The man on horseback was, of course, Mason Wolfe, and as he passed, the throng began chanting "The King of Israel! Blessed is he who comes in the name of the Lord."

Once the procession had crossed the valley they began to climb uphill. As it neared the great gate, the crowd continued to grow as more people in the city hurried to learn what was happening. "Who is this?" some questioned. Others shouted Wolfe's name while more and more took up the chant.

"The King of Israel! The King of Israel! The Messiah! Hosanna to the son of David!" The chief priests stood atop the wall and were moved with indignation. Had it not been their expectation that the High Priest alone would be the one at Wolfe's side when he was proclaimed Messiah? Then who were these usurpers now attending him?

The sound of a news helicopter above broke through the din and Brendan noticed more television cameras, not just hand held units, but also others that had apparently been installed on the gate for the occasion. "It looks like the whole world must be watching this," he said to John as he motioned toward the cameras.

"At least everyone who is awake," John agreed.

Tom Bertoldi was awed how magnificent Wolfe appeared astride the great horse. "Is there anything this guy can't do?" he said. "Bagnozzi ought to have stayed to see this," he added, not knowing that Bagnozzi had pleaded to stay, but Brendan had sent him back to Rome at first light.

Finally, the rider came alongside Brendan's group. Neither Enoch nor Elijah had revealed just how or when they would confront the false messiah and for the moment they stood and watched the rider pass. It was only as Wolfe drew even with Brendan's group that they thought to take notice of Wolfe's entourage. That group caused as much a sensation as the appearance of Wolfe himself.

Immediately behind Wolfe came none other than Scorfazza, dressed in the pope's white robes. Brendan Shea's robes, thought John. Walking beside him in scarlet was her Eminence Cardinal Eckhardt. Brendan recognized the Tibetan Dalai Lama and the Archbishop of Canterbury. Then came a feathered witch doctor and a famous American television evangelist. Everyone in Wolfe's parade seemed to be a religious leader of some sort. Since Father Bagnozzi was not with the little group, no one with Brendan recognized the face of Father Michael Bern as he followed behind the greater lights.

Once the last dignitaries had passed, the security people relaxed and permitted the crowd to close in behind the official procession. Pushing and shouting, the unstoppable throng streamed up the great staircase as if under pressure in a firehose. Brendan's group was swept through the ancient gate with Enoch and Elijah in the lead. Minutes later they were thrust into the gathering multitude on the wide plaza surrounding the Temple. Wolfe could not be seen, but all the religious leaders who had followed him through the gate appeared to take up positions on the raised porch along one side of the temple. The two prophets led their small group away from the Golden Gate and across the temple platform, finally stopping about fifty feet from the place where Scorfazza stood waiting.

When the huge plaza on the temple mount had become jammed with both the worshipping and the curious crowd the Dalai Lama stepped up to a high podium. The diminutive leader of the world's Tibetan Buddhists waited. The noise carried on a few minutes before a hush rippled across and engulfed the mount.

"The Fifth Buddha," he said speaking softly into the microphone. Then he turned and bowed to the rear. From his position next to the Lama, the Ayatollah Tabibi, in his flowing robes and turban, moved to the podium and addressed his Moslem brothers around the world.

"The Imam Mahdi," he announced.

"The God Krishna has returned," declared a smiling Hindu Maharishi in his colored robes. The Maharishi took his place next to the other leaders as the assembled people of Jerusalem waited to see if another herald would rise to the microphone. A cheer of recognition went up as they recognized the tall straight form of Rabbi and High Priest Ezekiel ben Jacob. He raised a hand to still the applause but the demonstration continued.

"Is there any title this monster will not take to himself?" Monsignor Bertoldi shouted into Brendan's ear as the crowd whooped enthusiastically. Brendan was attending less to the acclamations than to Enoch and Elijah who stood immediately in front of him. He felt an interior assurance that both calmed and energized him; the same assurance that had so often reminded him that the Holy Spirit was in control of events. He watched the two prophets because, despite his confidence in the outcome, he did not know how things would develop. This was not his day, Brendan understood, but theirs.

"Daughters and Sons of Abraham," the rabbi said softly, causing the cheers to quickly subside. Then drawing himself straighter still, he thundered, "The Anointed of God!".

The crowd began to shout "Messiah" and "King of Israel." Louder and louder they screamed, some taking up the chant of "Wolfe! Wolfe! Wolfe!" Finally, the white robed and capped figure of John XXIV, bishop of Rome and leader of Roman Catholics—as most men believed—stepped forward to make the final canonization of the new world teacher.

"Brothers and sisters!" Scorfazza said, appealing to acres of onlookers. "Brothers and sisters. Today you are witnesses to the greatest event in history. Eons ago our creator set this world in motion. From a lifeless earth came life, simple life. That life compounded itself, becoming more complex, and more, becoming conscious. And not just conscious, but conscious of itself, as if homing through the billions of years toward some far-off goal.

"Now one thing remains. All creation groans to see itself fully united with God. Fully become God. So we witness the first God-Man. My friends, behold our elder brother, the Christ, the Son of the living God, Mason Wolfe."

At once, the wild applause resumed; cheering and shouts. Then as Scorfazza stepped to one side of the podium, he bowed his head and dropped to one knee. Slowly, at first, those near him did likewise. Brendan watched the impostor Scorfazza and the first few dignitaries give their choreographed homage to the long prophesied antichrist. Then Wolfe came into view and those nearest who still stood seemed suddenly pressed down to the ground. The same force passed across the crowded temple mount as a great wave. Unstoppable, irresistible, the newspapers would later describe it. Members of the press, usually aloof from events, found themselves on their knees, lest they should be unable to remain upright at all.

"Save us," a voice cried out. "Son of David, have mercy on us!"

Mason Wolfe gazed across the mount at a sea of kneeling and prostrate worshippers, but distinct islands of persons who remained standing marred his pleasure. Wolfe saw a few isolated individuals dotted here and there. Standing far to one side, to Brendan's left, stood several robed monks, who Brendan recognized as his former monastic hosts. As Wolfe scanned the offenders, his eye was drawn to his right where he saw, standing immediately behind Scorfazza, the straight lean figure of Father Michael Bern. Father Bertoldi caught his breath at the seeming defiance of one of Wolfe's own entourage, scarcely realizing that he, Bertoldi, was himself still on his own feet. In holding his ground, Bern not only withheld homage, but revealed himself as traitor and spy.

In a control room miles away an irritated news director spoke aloud at the image of Wolfe on his monitors: "Stop looking away, you jerk." The planners had assumed that dissenters would be on the Temple Mount that morning, but under no circumstances were their pictures to be broadcast. "How in hell," he shouted to his assistant as he pointed at the picture of Bern, "are we supposed to keep the shot off that idiot when Wolfe is staring at him." The director was about to switch to a longer shot showing both men when Wolfe finally turned back to the front and faced his audience.

After the momentary distraction, Wolfe smoothed over the interruption and returned to the soothing fatherly manner that had become his comforting trademark. Wolfe spoke softly but firmly as he denounced the secularization of society and popular notions of the separation of church and state. He explained that such movements had once served their purpose.

"When we were divided," he explained, "we were divided by politics, divided by color, and especially by religion. But that time is past and we are one. As a sign of that oneness, all the leaders of the world's religions have joined in a synthesis of worship in which we recognize our own divinity. You know how reluctantly I have accepted this burden as firstborn of the dead. While I am the embodiment of that divinity, in truth I am your elder brother, and it is my greatest desire that each of you shall join me. Peace be with you all, my brothers and sisters." Wolfe began to turn and step from the podium when a shout clearly caught his attention.

"Oh no you don't," said the director to no one in particular, as he signaled to cut the outgoing signal.

"Mason Wolfe!" The booming voice was Elijah's and it immediately caught Wolfe's attention. "Mason Wolfe!" the prophet repeated even more loudly as every eye fell upon him. "You have sold yourself to do evil in the eyes of the Lord. As the Lord, the God of Israel, lives, whom I serve, there will be neither dew nor rain in these years except at my word."

Before Elijah spoke, GDA guards had already appeared from every corner and moved to arrest those self-identified rebels who had remained standing during the speech. Michael Bern was the first to be handcuffed and taken into custody. In ten days he would be brought out as Wolfe's first public execution, marking the beginning of a great persecution that would eventually dwarf all the murders by all the tyrants that had ever lived. Mason Wolfe faced the little group and glared. He recognized Brendan Shea and this time Wolfe seemed not at all surprised at his appearance.

"Take these men," said Wolfe pointing toward Elijah, "and keep them separate." A dozen guards moved toward them as the crowd opened a wide swath for the soldiers. Their captain approached Elijah, who was standing in front of the group, and Elijah warned him.

"Stay or you will die," said Elijah as he stepped backward. In response, the guard raised their weapons and moved toward Elijah and the others. Brendan felt the same tingling feeling he had experienced the evening before with the soldiers in the street and a moment later came the same blinding flash that consumed the captain and his men. The adoring crowd turned instantly into a terrorized stampede as they ran screaming toward the many exits from the temple mount. At the same time, a larger contingent of soldiers rushed through the thinning crowd near the podium toward Brendan's group. Again the air charged, and the fire fell as the lead group of more than twenty men died on their feet.

Finally, the moving mass of soldiers stopped and looked to where Mason Wolfe stood watching. Wolfe nodded. Go on. The soldiers started to obey. Brendan thought he felt the first prickle in the air as he stepped out from the group and shouted at the soldiers: "Stop!" The soldiers did stop; and Brendan continued, "If you do not fear God, then fear for your lives, for you will die if you take another step. You cannot harm us, but you can join us." Brendan came forward and climbed up the steps. He shouted to those that remained of the crowd, those curious and brave enough to stay and see what might happen next.

"Men of Israel! I am Brendan Shea, Bishop of Rome. You know whom I serve: Jesus Christ, the true Son of God, who was crucified in this city and in three days rose from the dead. This day the power of evil is loosed upon you." Brendan turned to his right where Mason Wolfe still stood watching from a distance. "Wolfe, your time is short, make what you will of it, for soon the Son of Man will come with the clouds of heaven and slay you with his sword."

Then he looked to the false pope: "It is not too late for you, Cardinal Scorfazza. Let another slave be the voice of hell. You come with us."

Scorfazza seemed momentarily torn in his loyalties. His pleasure at seeing the guards move to arrest Shea had disintegrated as quickly as the guards who had attempted to apprehend the young pope. Scorfazza looked to an angry, defiant and still proud Mason Wolfe and saw only opportunity. He was indeed divided, but not between Wolfe and Shea, but between Wolfe and himself.

"All hail, Lord Wolfe," declared Scorfazza as he raised his hands in praise to the ruler of the earth. "For now at least," he said to himself.

Brendan stepped down to the pavement. His little group then left by the north entrance to the mount. Most of the spectators moved out of their path as they came down the long stairs to the street level, but still there were many who ached to hear another message, a message that did not center upon the man-god Mason Wolfe.

"I told my sister that this man Wolfe would make himself out to be a god!" said a young Palestinian woman as she rushed up to the two prophets with Brendan. She was a Christian, but her sister, who came up silently beside her, was a Moslem. The Moslem teenager was shaking and appeared to have been in tears. She had come to the Temple Mount out of curiosity, just in time to hear her own spiritual leader proclaim Wolfe as the long-awaited world teacher. "She does not believe in Jesus as we do, but she now understands that President Wolfe is from the evil one."

"Look at me girl," Enoch said to her as he took the young woman's downcast chin in his firm hand, raising it to his face. "Do you know me?" he demanded. The Palestinian tried to look away but Enoch held her, with his eyes as well as his grip. "I was old when your father Abraham was born. I am a servant of the Ancient of Days, Father, Son and Holy Spirit. I offer you one hope, and that only for your soul. Do you believe me?" The Moslem stopped trying to pull away and let her eyes remain on the old man. Enoch turned the Palestinian girl's face toward Brendan and said to her: "Then do whatever he tells you."

Brendan put his hand on her arm and guided her away from the others. Brendan talked with her quietly. The girl spoke several times in response, then Brendan dismissed her with a hand upraised in blessing. The Palestinian waved to her sister to join her and they walked away together.

"Well, sister, do you believe me now?" asked the first teenager.

"I do. And I'm glad"

"What did he tell you?"

"Everything will be fine," she answered, then more quietly, "But he also said we need to be ready to die, maybe soon."

Brendan's party would not arrive back at the stone house for many hours as similar scenes played out again and again. It was mostly Jews that came; from the ultra-orthodox to those purely secular Jews, more than Brendan could count. To most he promised the crown of martyrdom. And it was a relief compared to the hopelessness each had felt growing inside. These, even though they had fallen before Wolfe's face, had felt their hearts leap at the appearance of Brendan, Enoch and Elijah. Most had thought themselves utterly alone, misfits in a world in love with Mason Wolfe. They had despaired almost to the point of death. Now they could rejoice at the same fate.

Brendan, too, was strengthened by the encounters. Only once during that day was he fearful. As he reached the bottom of the temple steps, an angry couple ran up, screaming profanities in his face. Brendan first panicked with horror, looking first at Elijah on one side, and Enoch on the other. It quickly became clear to Brendan that no heavenly fire would fall, so he faced the angry pair and smiled widely; so widely that they managed but one further snarl and then stalked away.

"No heavenly protection from insults, I take it?" Brendan observed.

"Perhaps, if your Holiness wishes . . . ." said Elijah with seriousness.

"No, please," Brendan said just as another man sought him out.

Chapter Thirteen

And when you see the abomination of desolation . . .
standing in the holy place . . . there shall then be
great tribulation such as has not been since the
beginning of the world . . .

—Matthew 24:15, 21

Back at the old stone house, John Daniels wanted to know what would come next. He had drawn strength from what he had seen and now seemed to fear death less than he feared uncertainty. Still he had to ask: "Father, are we going to die soon?"

"No, John. Not soon. The Holy Spirit has begun the last great harvest. The words of Enoch and Elijah will gather them in, and we must be ready to feed them when they come to us. There will be no quick way through for the members of this household."

Elijah sat down by John and explained further: "This house is a castle in a storm that will cease only when the one who commands the wind and waves returns. You saw today that the Lord will not permit any harm to our mission until it is complete. Not one of us would be safe until morning if that extraordinary grace were withdrawn. If you are with Enoch; if you are with me, then you are safe. If you are in this sanctuary, you are safe. But nowhere else. Do you understand?" John Daniels nodded yes, but he would spend all of the next three and a half years learning what it meant.

"Now that we are out of the monastery," asked Bertoldi, "how will we communicate with the outside? Surely Wolfe will know our every move."

"Come in here," Brendan said to him, motioning toward a doorway they had not yet explored. "Not all of our assistance is from heaven. See what we have been provided." The small room was full of communications gear; satellite radio, computers and even video equipment. "John," he said, gesturing for John step over and to look inside, "I am told that tomorrow a visitor will arrive from America." Brendan stepped inside and swept his hand toward the stacks of gadgetry. "He will begin your instructions in its use."

The communications room was the work of that American, George Christmas, a former marine, widower and self-made billionaire who made his personal fortune building communications satellites. The president and sole stockholder of Star-Net Communications still could not say whether he had a dream or a vision, but it had been ten years since he awoke and resolved to make possible the little room in the stone house in Jerusalem.

Christmas started by designing unused frequencies into his satellites—channels that could be secretly activated at a later date. He buried signals inside commercial broadcast bands like needles in haystacks; or fleas on a dog. Christmas built the strongest encryption algorithms on the planet to insure that even if the signals were discovered, they would never be deciphered.

Then he shielded his satellites from every sort of interference. Only modern military satellites were so hardened and therefore able to withstand the most intense man-made and natural electro-magnetic radiation.

Having done all those things to make each machine reliable and impenetrable, George Christmas overbuilt in sheer numbers so that the signals could be shifted from one orbital platform to another automatically as needed. Most of his cash reserves went into his secret systems and the public image of his company suffered irreparable damage as many of his satellites time and again rocketed into geosynchronous orbit only to go mysteriously silent. George would awaken them at the appointed time.

Late the next evening, a boy—thin, scrawny and looking about twelve years old—appeared from a cellar door. Yussef was Mrs. Habash's only child. In fact, the boy was sixteen, a devout Catholic like his mother, and an experienced sneak. The boy led a bewildered, blinking George Christmas up the old stairway and into the light and spacious room. After a three day absence the boy was obviously anxious to be home and hugged his mother accordingly. "How is our tunnel rat?" Elijah said, as he too embraced the dusty young man and then introduced him to Brendan, John and Tom Bertoldi. Yussef was not surprised to see the visitors, but nonetheless, he came close to tears when Brendan was introduced to him.

"Holy Father," Yussef said as he tried to kneel at Brendan's feet. Brendan raised him up.

"You are a brave soul," Brendan said. "I will want to hear about your traveling, Yussef."

Yussef had just returned from relatives in the city, Christian Arabs; and loyal to Brendan Shea. There he had made contact with Christmas. Yussef was able to come and go through a tunnel under the ancient house. His cousins lived at the other end of the tunnel, several hundred feet away. If not for the tunnel, anyone who left the house without the protection of Enoch or Elijah would surely be arrested before they could walk across the street. A man might get into the old stone house, but he could not otherwise get out. Yussef's importance was chiefly as a guide, smuggling people in and out.

The next few days were a blur for John. The rich American with the festive name undertook John's training, gladly and patiently. John so quickly mastered the use of the equipment that George convinced John he been all wrong in undertaking a restaurant career. If George knew of John's career as a terrorist bomber, he made no mention of it.

"You're a natural with these machines," the square-jawed executive remarked with genuine praise. "I could use more like you at Star-Net," he said. John was happy, not simply for the praise, but more for this opportunity to serve Brendan and the Church in some meaningful way. Sometimes he had felt like he was doing nothing but hanging on. "I take that back, John," George continued, "We don't need you at Star-Net. We need you here. I can't stay here long and between my visits you will keep all this going."

Day after day, Enoch and Elijah went to the temple to preach. The people came too, even though most understood the danger even in listening to the two witnesses. Some were in sympathy with the prophets. Others who came were simply more curious than afraid, and others would not be kept away for any reason, for they came to ask the old prophets to heal them.

Enoch explained their mission to the crowds: "Mason Wolfe has been sent by the evil one to lead men into error. Elijah and I may look like other men, but God has preserved us in a hidden place where we knew not the suffering of men. Now we are sent to you to oppose the lies of this sorcerer Wolfe and to proclaim to you the truth of the Almighty."

Elijah would set out the Law of Moses to the Israeli Jews and they would understand as they had never understood before. He would show them from those same scriptures how Jesus of Nazareth is the Messiah. Then bit by bit, the scales fell from Israel's eyes and the Jews believed. As always, Enoch and Elijah directed the converts to Brendan Shea, whose underground Church stretched to handle the hundreds, sometimes thousands, of new Christians each day.

Wolfe did not sleep while the Church grew. As befitting his twin capitols, Wolfe made Jerusalem and Rome the most magnificent cities on earth. Rome had become the center of commerce and political power; Jerusalem the seat of spiritual authority and power. In every city and region there was set up a place, a lodge or church or synagogue, where an image of the man-god, Mason Wolfe, would be displayed. Eventually every man and woman must come before the image and swear allegiance to Wolfe and take a mark on their hand or head, without which mark, nothing could be bought or sold.

This was the new rite of Scorfazza's church that Brendan and the others knew was coming. The well-crafted rite was as majestic as a Cathedral High Mass; the music as moving as the best movie score. The composer claimed he had collaborated with the spirits of J.S. Bach as well as an award-winning, but deceased composer for several animated Disney movies. The rite would go far to satisfy that deep human need for worship, while implicitly denying the divinity of Jesus and expressly recognizing Mason Wolfe as the Christ. At the terminus of the spectacle, the music would swell and fill every space, as each initiate received the mark on the forehead or right hand. The rubrics allowed for either, but many would take the mark on the forehead to accentuate their loyalty to the new order and to Mason Wolfe. Afterward, there could be no question about where a man stood.

The new rite or the Initiation, as it was called, was unveiled first in Jerusalem. The separating veil in the great temple had been removed and there was set up in the sacred place, the Holy of Holies, a golden throne of Olympian proportions, ten feet high at the seat alone. The participants, robed in white, filled all the temple space before the great throne as the priests made their entrance.

Outside, along the north colonnade of the temple, Brendan Shea worked with Enoch and Elijah as they had been doing every day for the last week. The prophets preached, and then condemned, in turn. Their hearers had grown daily, so that Brendan and Tom Bertoldi could give little more than a blessing and a word of encouragement before sending the Jewish converts to a growing network of both priests and laymen who would instruct and prepare them for Baptism. But today, because of what was happening inside the temple, was different.

"We go up before the throne of the god who gives us joy and invites us to become one with him," intoned the master celebrant as the ceremony began.

"As He is, we may now become," came the reply from the priests.

GDA security men were startled when Brendan and the prophets entered by a side door they thought locked. Elijah gently waved a hand and recognition registered on the faces of the guards. They made no move against the men of God who stood quietly to watch the Initiation. The service, both in words and song, sounded one theme, over and over: infinite humankind, infinite in potential. Let us wake to our divinity, the soothing song assured them; then join the elder brother, Wolfe, and become gods ourselves.

The sound of the last hymn echoed briefly through the temple and died. The quiet pause lengthened, but no one moved. The initiates did not stir, but seemed fixed on the great throne. Then when it seemed the silence could not go on, there was a change. Brendan wasn't certain whether the lights had begun to dim or only seemed so, now that the silence was absolute. Brendan felt it before he could hear it. The sensation reminded him of lying in bed at night as a boy. The approach of the nightly freight train always began as a tickle or rumble deep inside. No matter how many times the train came, he never recognized the initial rumbling for what it was. Instead, it filled him slowly, growing, until finally the thought would form: the train. Funny, he thought, that most words evoked a picture in his mind, but "train" always formed a sound in his brain. This sound was like that. So slight at first; so long in coming; and finally, so intrusive a thorn as to drive out all others.

The shock caused a collective intake of breath. From the corner of his eye, Brendan noticed several initiates faint away, but like the rest, his eyes fixed on the figure that seemed to materialize before their eyes. The giant would have been thirty feet tall had he stood, but the golden, highly muscled figure was seated on the great throne.

"What is it?" John whispered to Brendan. "A statue of Wolfe?"

"Statues don't breathe, John," Brendan answered as the man of gold began to scan the interior of the holy place. More initiates fainted as the gaze fell on them. Then the eyes looked at Brendan. Brendan thought he saw recognition. How is he doing it? This time there was no shock, no momentary loss of composure from the golden Wolfe. There was only malice; malice that penetrated Brendan's mind with the power of a physical assault. Brendan almost staggered. Then he said to John, "Don't look at it."

The first initiates came forward and stood a few yards in front of the giant, bowing their heads, not daring to raise their eyes. The giant still looked out at the great mass of people, then finally he looked down on the little men and women at his feet and spoke in a voice like thunder. Like a beast, he sounds, thought Monsignor Bertoldi. "Worship!" the monster bellowed.

Each initiate, as if flattened by the voice itself, pressed himself face down on the ground before the beast. They lay still for a few moments and then the priests came and raised each one to his feet. As they returned to their places, the mark—which had not been present when each initiate came forward—was now clearly visible.

Brendan had not known what form the mark might take. Some thought it would be a name or a number; or perhaps a special symbol. But this was just a black stain on the forehead. No more than an inch across, the unholy stigmata marked an irrevocable divide. To refuse it, Brendan assumed would mean death; to take it, he knew also, would be worse. The next group came forward, then the third, until only a few robed initiates yet remained to prostrate themselves before the god of the new age.

Throughout the ritual, Enoch and Elijah, Brendan and the others had only waited. No preaching once we are inside, Enoch had said, for no hearts would be changed once before the beast. So they watched quietly as hundreds of men and women offered adoration and thereby purchased the seal that would feed their bodies and damn their souls.

Then three robed figures came forward. It was for these that Brendan had come. There was the Abbot from the monastery that had hidden Brendan for three years. Brendan had stayed apart from most of the monks, but the Abbot he knew well. The Abbot was an able, practical administrator, and Brendan often reflected that the Abbot might make a better Pope and Brendan a more monkish monk. The young monk who kept the gate was also there; and also Father Michael Bern. All had been imprisoned since the day they had failed to kneel before Wolfe.

Like those who preceded them, they had been instructed that they needed only recognize Wolfe as Messiah and pay him that worship due the man-god. Soon they could share in his divinity. Take the mark and live; no matter what your life was before. Take the mark and be made a new creation. Reject it and die.

John Daniels stood next to Brendan. Until this moment, he wished it were he that stood at the feet of the golden beast. I would not bow, John said to himself. I would die and be glad to leave this wretched world. But now John looked at the young monk and saw that he trembled before the giant. The monk convulsed as a sob went through him. John was suddenly sick with fear; fear for the monk and sick with disgust at his own pride. The beast looked at each man. Its monstrous face seemed to take on an expression of both hatred and satisfaction as it slowly spoke the command: "Worship!" Michael Bern showed no fear, but stiffened his back and stared straight into its face. The young monk trembled more and turned his eyes to the ground, but he did not move.

The Abbot lay flat on his face, as did the hundreds before him. The priest had to raise him from the floor and led him back to his place. Brendan saw no hint of recognition in the Abbot's eyes as he went past him. Up close, the irregular black mark on the Abbot's forehead was raised and blisterous, like some dark leprosy.

The beast looked down at the defiant Bern and the young monk. The monk had regained his composure and stood squarely alongside the priest. His decision now past, he seemed fearful no more. The golden beast spoke again, but quietly and facing the audience.

"You must understand, brothers, what has happened today. You have each taken that first step. This initiation is being repeated in every land around this globe, and soon . . ." The golden Wolfe paused. "Soon every man, every woman, every child, shall join with me as with one mind. We shall leave behind this vale of tears and lift ourselves to godhood: to a new level of existence."

Then the voice rose, and no longer gentle: "But that will not happen, brothers. It can not happen, until we are all one. These who have chosen to stay behind," the monster said, again looking down again at the two, "are an impurity in the body of humankind; a decay and a corruption so hideous that for their sake, and ours, they will be sent to another plane of existence. There they may come to see what they cannot now see. One day they will be ready to join us, but not now.

Then the monster again looked down at the two rebels and spoke as a judge: "You priest, and you monk, this world now ejects you. Learn well."

As the beast spoke the last words, he vanished from the throne. GDA security men immediately bound the hands of the two and led them out the east entrance of the temple and roughly pulled them to their right, leading them onto the plaza on the south side of the temple.

Wolfe's judgment would be swift. For several years, Wolfe had been processing his enemies through formal, but phony, show trials. Once convicted of treason, the inevitable punishment was death. Now, by means of the temple ritual, the charade of a trial was eliminated in favor of a bright line test: bow to Wolfe's image and take the mark. Or die.

Wolfe had always been a student and enthusiast of the French Revolution and, early on, he reintroduced capital punishment by guillotine. Publicly, Wolfe lamented its use, but defended the device as being the most humane. Privately, Wolfe was happy to trade the physical pain of other means of execution for the emotional terror of the guillotine. Besides, his torturers usually took some time alone with the condemned before removing his head.

Michael Bern and the monk stood between the temple and the guillotine, where they waited. The temple mount was filled with the new initiates as well as other visitors already in the temple area. Brendan and his company were able to come very near to the place of execution, because the guards, especially those who had seen the inexplicable power of Enoch and Elijah, would not lightly make any move against them.

Michael Bern and the monk were pushed up several steps to an elevated platform. Bern looked peaceful, his face turned upward in obvious prayer. Tom Bertoldi and John Daniels stood on either side of Brendan. The two prophets watched impassively from just behind Brendan. Then one guard spoke to Father Bern and Bern moved to place himself in the hellish device. John started to weep silently, for both Bern and himself. He wished it were himself on the guillotine.

Monsignor Bertoldi moved his head to Brendan's ear and spoke matter of factly, "The first of the many martyrs of the new age, Brendan." Then he noticed Brendan's cheek was bright red; his whole face flushed even more than usual. "With what?" Bertoldi thought, "Rage?"

Brendan suddenly turned around to face Elijah.

"I need him, Elijah. I need you to save both him and the monk."

"Then do it," Elijah said as he nodded toward the platform.

Brendan pushed hard into the crowd and wormed his way to a corner of the platform. Bern slipped his neck into the notch beneath the unused blade and one guard stooped to secure it in place. As Brendan neared the steps a strong hand took his shoulder. "Let go, son," Brendan warned and the guard fell back. He had seen Brendan before. The next hand did not let go. Brendan felt the static rise and then the hand and its owner were gone in the flash. Another soldier three feet away was also consumed, but Brendan was unharmed. Amid the screams and shouts Brendan mounted the steps and freed Bern. Father Bern, who had so serenely accepted his fate, now moved reluctantly as Brendan pulled him away from the guillotine. No other GDA soldier moved to interfere as Brendan ordered Bern and the monk off the platform.

"We're leaving," he shouted to the others. The crowd parted hastily and the company, plus two, marched quickly off the mount, through the narrow streets of the Moslem Quarter and on to the stone house. This time they did not stop along the way. No one spoke until they had regained the cool safety of the old house. Mrs. Habash greeted the two newcomers with a quiet satisfied smile, as if the addition of two more houseguests was a gift from God. She set Yussef quickly to work with plates and chairs and soon Father Bern and the young monk were eating the first real meal they had seen since their capture after Wolfe's triumphal entry.

"How will we get enough food into the house to feed everyone here?" John asked, thinking about the head count at the Habash household, which continued to rise.

"Enoch, my brother," Elijah said, "Would you mind stopping at the market on your way home from the temple tomorrow?"

The older man did not look up, but responded shortly, "And what do you suppose I will use for money?" Wolfe had succeeded in pulling the financial plug on the Catholic pope as well as on every one connected with him, whether inside Wolfe's prisons or not. It was an easy task now that the use of paper money had been phased out.

"You see that refrigerator over there?" Enoch said to Tom Bertoldi. "Elijah has always had this arrangement with God. He travels around the country, challenging and anger-ing all the powers that be; then they spend all their time trying to kill him. In exchange, he gets fed. Since we have been here, that machine over there is somehow always full of food. I don't know what we'll do if Wolfe finds how we get electric power in here, but I'll guess that refrigerator would keep on running even if we pulled the plug." John walked over and pulled open the refrigerator door, and wondered that he hadn't noticed before.

After the meal Brendan asked the prophet: "Elijah, what are your plans?"

The rough prophet stood up at his place and looked to each of them as he spoke: "To preach to the Children of Israel. The time of the gentiles is ended and we have already seen that the time for Israel to believe is now. They know that this man Wolfe is not their Messiah. What we saw today was a complete fraud. That giant apparition was a mere device of men, I am sure. Even the seemingly universal acceptance of Wolfe's mark—saving, of course our two brothers here—was orchestrated. No, I have come for the Jews, and even though the whole world follows Wolfe, they will not."

"Enoch?" Brendan asked.

"I will join Elijah when I am here in Jerusalem, but I go to the whole earth and my time is short. Only now am I ready to set out on that mission, for the addition of Father Bern and Brother . . . "

"David," offered the young monk.

"Yes, David. Holy Father, today you took these two from the beast's mouth; not for their own sakes, for both were content to leave us as martyrs. I would ask then a favor, Brendan Shea. Bless this monk David and send him with me on my mission."

Brendan agreed, realizing only then why he had shouted in the temple courtyard that morning. He needed Bern and the monk David, not for his own work but to send as tested companions to Enoch and Elijah. That evening both were ordained as bishops, successors to the apostles, and empowered to ordain others to the priesthood. Then they prayed and sang hymns into the night. In the morning Brendan blessed the four and they left.

Brendan knew that the future was to be filled with both sorrow and glory. Only now had Wolfe begun to show his teeth and it was in the tribulation to follow that the false would be separated from the true. He thought of the Abbott, and began to offer a prayer for him; then stopped, filled with grief and knowing that no prayer would bring back any man who had taken the mark. He is already dead, Brendan realized, even while he yet lives. Until now, a man was never finally lost until death. But from now on, anyone who worshipped the image of the beast Wolfe was forever damned. That was the thought that energized Brendan Shea for the next three years.

Constantly, in every way, he encouraged the church to remain strong in the trial. And he knew the trial would come not only from persecution, but from unprecedented natural disasters, for he had been given a glimpse of the future and saw that the plagues recited in the scriptures were more than symbols.

The drought worsened. In Israel, true to Elijah's promise, there had not fallen a single drop of rain. The poor, even the ones who had taken the mark, were the first to starve, as the earth and its vegetation dried up.

Then, without warning, came the solar flare. While half the world slept, the other half, western Europe, Africa and the Americas, were seared by the greatest burst of radiation ever recorded. People exposed in tropical latitudes suffered hideous sunburns in the short time it took to get to shelter. Paper caught fire and then the grass. Before the flare subsided the dried grasslands burned. In eastern Europe and the Middle East, sleepers awoke to find the dawning sun blazing like noonday. The resultant winds blew the fires to distant places such that in the end it seemed that neither grass nor food crops could remain anywhere. The smoke of the burning darkened the sun by day and by night the haze turned the moon to a red disk, dark and deep, like blood.

But worse came in the days to follow. While most had survived the initial sunburn, only those who were well shielded by earth, rock, concrete or steel were spared the damage of radiation, which penetrated wood and glass. Millions sickened and died within weeks.

Throughout the turmoil, Enoch and Elijah continued journeying to every corner of both Israel and the world. While Mason Wolfe controlled the media, he could not prevent news of the two prophets from spreading, for everywhere they went, they worked marvels of feeding the hungry crowds and healing the sick as Jesus had. When the crowds came, they were turned to the crucified and resurrected Christ and away from Mason Wolfe; and always they bid the converts to follow Brendan Shea.

They came by the millions, and having come, they would never bow to the golden Wolfe; never take the mark. Most followers of Brendan Shea suffered for their faith, but the fortunes of one follower, a secret follower, rose spectacularly after the tragic solar flare.

George was waiting nervously in the green room when the assistant producer of the *Julie!* show stuck her head in the door. "It's time, Mr. Christmas. Follow me." George was relieved to be getting it over with. The usually self-assured entrepreneur had spent a lifetime in the television business, but not in front of the camera. He was more nervous than he thought he would be.

"My next guest is the President of Star-Net Communications. You would not be watching this program if not for the foresight of our guest. Until the rest of the world recovers from the great flare, Mr. George Christmas is sole owner of the only working civilian communications satellites in orbit. Let's welcome this remarkable man."

George need not have been anxious, for even the most restive guest was soon at ease with Julie Dermott. Without getting into the true purpose of the Star-Net network of satellites, George explained his unusual dedication to building satellites that could survive even the most rigorous trials in space. Competitors had considered him a crank. Many still did, but now that he was a popular hero, they had to admit was a lucky crank.

"I guess the television networks have to pay whatever price you name, right George?" Julie quipped.

"On no, Julie," George said, looking momentarily wounded. George had charged no more for the use of his channels than he had charged before he owned a monopoly. Julie winced as she saw his pained expression. Then she changed the subject.

"I notice, George, that you have not yet been through the Initiation. When is it?" Julie said to someone off-camera, "When is it that we need to have that done? Three weeks? You know, I was going to go right away. I would do anything to support Mr. Wolfe, but every time I've scheduled, something gets in the way."

"I've been the same, Julie. You can imagine that I've been traveling a lot, but I go to the temple soon."

George's time on the air was quickly over, but he was not finished with his business. The producer came to him after the show and led him to see Julie. Julie asked George to have a seat while she poured coffee. "Like a cup, George? Nobody here can make a pot to suit me, so I brew my own. So tell me why you sent me this note."

"I needed to talk to you privately." George began slowly. He told her about John Daniels: about how John was also healed the same night that she was. George told her how John had come to believe in Brendan Shea.

"Brendan Shea was there the night you were healed. You know that, Julie. I know you believe Mason Wolfe healed you. He did not." Julie knew that John had tried to save her from the explosion, but she could only resist the idea that Brendan Shea had given her back her life. Everything that had happened since that horrible night seemed explainable only by what Wolfe had done.

"I know you are Catholic, Julie. Surely you are offended by this thug, Scorfazza, who pretends to be Pope while destroying all that is good. When you go to your Initiation you must not bow to the image. You must not take the mark, because when you do, you make yourself the enemy of God. On that day you will die the death that does not end." Julie raised her hand and stood up.

"Please leave, Mr. Christmas," Julie said dully. George left.

Mason Wolfe would never learn of George Christmas' appeal to Julie Dermott, nor would it matter, for George would soon be out of the tyrant's reach. But Wolfe had now to deal with another problem, far bigger than he had ever anticipated. On a practical level, the vast harvest of new Christians was forcing him to re-evaluate his plan of systematic persecution. Further, the loss of so many to the side of his enemy sent him into blind, wild rage. Under the current rules, Wolfe's professional murderers were hard pressed to meet the demand.

They grew first tired of the killing, and then, overwhelmed. Soon it was apparent that another solution must be found. Wolfe's initial answer to the problem was a program of mass execution by use of chemical weapons. He would reserve the guillotine for special cases.

Releasing nerve gas over the camps seemed an easy way to kill every prisoner in a camp, but the plan was not without its own special problems. The initial trouble was in the burying of 100,000 bodies at one time, using backhoes and bulldozers. The strain on the workers was staggering; the task a hundred times worse than that faced by the Nazis. Then there came an unexpected shift in the wind that caused a 100,000 unintentional deaths in a nearby city and finally pushed Wolfe to what he called his "Thermal Intensive" solution.

The first experiment required three miles of chain link fence surrounding a circular area one mile across. A tall tower was erected in the center of the circle topped by a platform appearing much like a stage at an outdoor concert. GDA troops transported 250,000 people to the site. They used buses, trucks and trains; and for two hours the prisoners were unloaded at the gates and ordered to move into the center, near the platform.

Almost all were religious and political prisoners who had been arrested for their opposition to Mason Wolfe or their refusal to make the new worship and take the mark. The remainder, ironically, were genuine criminals: robbers, thieves, drug dealers and murderers; former inmates from various state and federal prisons. These were made trustees, prisoners who were given responsibilities and privileges denied the others. The trustees were left at the gates and given weapons. "Do this task well," they were told, "and you will be free after today." They were ordered to shoot anyone who approached the gates from inside.

"Keep the guns for yourselves!" shouted the last of the GDA troops as they drove away quickly.

A half-mile away, at the center of the enclosure, a small man began to climb the stairway up the tower. The massive crowd began to notice the solo climber as shouts of "Brother Joe" rose up and thousands of arms began to point toward the figure as he labored toward the summit of the tower. After five minutes Joe Dupre, attorney and counselor at law, and founder of the *Prisoners of Christ* stood at the top, winded and puffing. The crowd grew silent as he caught his breath and straightened. Brother Joe began in a strong voice, but not a voice that might reach even halfway to the back of the assembly three hundred yards away. But it did not need to reach so far alone. He made the Sign of the Cross and spoke:

"Our Father, Who art in heaven, hallowed be thy name." Those near the tower crossed themselves and joined with the monk. "Thy Kingdom come, Thy will be done." Fifty thousand now prayed.

At the gates, the trustees shook their heads and wondered again about these Christians. One of them, however, was still trying to sort out his place in the chaos. Jimmy Young was the convicted mass murderer who had unwittingly helped to catapult Mason Wolfe to world power. His years on death row

had been bitter. Jimmy had always been taught that the
Catholic Church was a corruption of biblical Christianity, yet
Brendan Shea's Church was the only visible opposition to
Wolfe. His despair grew as the world separated into the two
camps of Mason Wolfe and Brendan Shea. Jimmy could never
believe in the enemy Wolfe, but neither could he consider the
alternative.

Jimmy's entire cellblock on death row had been emptied and he and his fellow killers transported to this piece of
fenced-in desert prairie. Jimmy laid the rifle against the
fence and looked toward the tower and the prisoners inside
the enclosure. Most of the other trustees, were now out of
hearing range, for they had started running into the desert
the moment the last GDA trucks were out of sight. It didn't
matter. None of the prisoners moved toward the gates.

Jimmy recognized the sound of the spreading prayer
as a quarter million souls joined in with Brother Joe: " . . . on
earth, as it is in heaven." Jimmy looked toward the top of the
fence. It wasn't that high. Jimmy began to climb the chain
link barrier. "Give us this day, our daily bread . . . ." Mason
Wolfe watched by satellite as his GDA general detonated the
thermonuclear device at Brother Joe's feet. The weapon
cleared an area ten times that enclosed by the fence, vaporizing the martyrs inside and catching even those trustees who
had been running away for five minutes.

Mason Wolfe read the follow-up reports at the table while his
Corrections Department Director sat waiting for his questions. "And the clean-up after sentence is carried out?"

"My Lord, other than the residual radioactivity, there
is no clean up; at any rate, nothing that cannot be plowed under after the plan is completed."

"Are you concerned about security if the prisoners
should become resistant."

"As you know we were very concerned at the first explosion. It took hours to unload the prisoners. From our experience in the camps, we did not expect resistance, but were

anxious about the possibility of panic, especially if they began to suspect the outcome."

"Did they suspect it?" asked Wolfe.

"Well yes, some did, but it did not matter. After the first test, we built a second enclosure upwind of the first. Half million, but it was the same. Once inside, somebody would start them off praying. With a million prisoners it took all day to unload and still they neither rebelled nor seemed to fear their fate."

"Alright, you will have all the resources you need, but I want this done in twelve to eighteen months. We should manage two executions a week, don't you think?"

"And if the nuclear testing schedule does not keep that pace?" asked the Director.

"I will authorize any further necessary requisitions from the arsenal," Wolfe assured him. "Anything else?" The Director shook his head and Wolfe dismissed him.

Chapter Fourteen

And he shall send his angels with a trumpet,
and a great voice: and they shall gather together
his elect from the four winds, from one end of
heaven to the other.
                                    —*Matthew 24:31*

In a moment, in the twinkling of an eye, at the
last trumpet: for the trumpet shall sound, and
the dead shall rise again incorruptible, and we
shall be changed.
                                    —*1 Corinthians 15:52*

George Christmas had felt dejected when he left the studio after his appearance on the *Julie!* show two weeks before. Meeting the young Julie Dermott in person had only made his failure seem a greater tragedy. He sent a message to Brendan Shea that night expressing his disappointment and begging the Pope's prayers for Julie and for himself. He knew his own time was at an end.

George dutifully put on the initiation robes, playing the good citizen to the very end. It had become customary for public figures to come forward early in the ceremonies, chiefly for the purpose of meeting television news deadlines. Nightly news broadcasts always-made mention of notable persons who had taken the mark on that particular day. When the first rank of initiates prostrated itself before the golden giant, one small woman remained standing. A shock went through the room as George—along with everyone else—recognized the popular Julie Dermott now standing alone and self-condemned. George was in the second group of initiates and he smiled as he came forward. His own faith had not wavered during these hard years, but he lived with the sorrow of knowing that his own son and daughter had taken the mark. Somehow the turning of this sweet soul back to the Lord and away from the demon Wolfe worked a miracle in his own spirit. George went to his death in peace, as did Julie and ten thousand others who had refused Wolfe's bargain that morning.

Brendan knew that the world was fast approaching an end-point. The final deadline for ritual acceptance of the mark was now past. The bank accounts of all who had not taken the mark were confiscated and no one without the mark could hold a job or buy and sell. Generous rewards motivated friends and relatives to report the dwindling numbers of free rebels. Most of those free men and women were followers of Brendan Shea, except for a significant number of Israeli Jews. Many Israelis had refused to appear for the temple ritual; so many that Wolfe had not yet moved against them. They had not taken the mark, but neither had they responded to Elijah's call.

Outside Israel, Enoch's work with David the monk came to an end as the deadline passed. Enoch rejoined Elijah and daily they would come to the temple mount together with Brendan Shea to preach the gospel of Jesus, the Jewish Messiah. The flow of converts from among the sons and daughters of Israel turned into a flood so great that neither Wolfe nor his troops could hope to control it.

Scorfazza trembled as he entered the anteroom of Wolfe's private suite at his Jerusalem Headquarters. A sulphurous fragrance hung in the air. The anti-pope had no power to withstand Wolfe's hellish rages, which had become more furious with recent setbacks. Religious and governmental leaders in Israel increasingly chafed against Wolfe's virtual takeover of the country and the Israeli people now largely rejected Wolfe as Messiah. Wolfe maintained a low military profile in Tel Aviv and Jerusalem. In the countryside, however, the massive, swelling GDA army was outgrowing its bases throughout Israel's central plain.

The drought foretold by Elijah continued. Famine and disease killed millions every month; even the mark of the beast could not save men where there was no food or medicine to buy. The horrendous accounts of death and torment disturbed Wolfe, not because of the human suffering, but because the messengers also brought reports of rebellion within formerly docile national governments.

Russia made the first independent moves. She began by gobbling up several of the lost soviet republics. Russia's digestion of its first Muslim state inflamed the Islamic nations, which were already resentful because of Wolfe's favorable treatment of Israel. Damascus and Cairo, Baghdad and Tehran, all rose as one, and declared independence from Wolfe and the global alliance. The threat of a resurrected Soviet Union woke a slumbering China. China quickly mobilized for war.

Now Scorfazza tried to steel himself as he was led into Wolfe's inner office, but he feared he would lose control of himself before the wrath of the Lord of the World. Now fear turned to puzzlement as a smiling and cordial Mason Wolfe invited Scorfazza to have a seat.

"Holy Father," Wolfe said with seeming respect, "Today we will be delivered from our nemesis. My Father has made known to me that Enoch and Elijah will be defeated this very day."

"How so, my Lord?" Scorfazza asked warily, still disbelieving in the affable image before his eyes.

Wolfe picked up the telephone. "Is the guard readied? Thank you," Wolfe laid down the phone. "Come with me and you will see the end of those so-called 'prophets' and also your Brendan Shea and that crucified master of his." Wolfe led the way out of the building as his aides joined them. Outside it was a bright and cloudless April morning. Wolfe imagined he felt some promise of moisture in the air, but the sky and the parched earth gave no such suggestion. The motorcade left immediately under the tight security provided by both GDA troops and Wolfe's personal guard. It was a short drive to the temple mount and Wolfe's entourage disembarked at the Golden Gate. Heavy-handed troops had cleared the street leading up to the gate and now proceeded to open a path to the mount itself where the throng listened to the words of Elijah.

"People of Israel, you would not be here if you did not reject the false messiah, Mason Wolfe. Your time is short and God is good, but He will not stay his judgment forever! For he is coming on the clouds of heaven and you will look upon him and weep because you rejected him. Choose now. Come and be baptized in the name of the Father and of his Son, Jesus Christ, and of the Holy Spirit" The stream of converts seemed endless and as each came forward, Enoch guided them to nearby fonts where Brendan Shea and others baptized them one by one.

Elijah did not stop speaking as Wolfe's guard found positions surrounding him. Some of the soldiers had seen the deadly power that protected these men and they understood how far one might go before inciting that power. Wolfe did not expect to deter the prophets, but the onlookers quickly moved back. Some feared the GDA troops, while others moved back lest the dreaded fire consume them when it fell upon the soldiers.

Enoch and Elijah stood alone in a wide circle of Wolfe's men as Mason Wolfe strode fearlessly into the circle. Scorfazza stood outside it, taking care to keep a safe distance from both Wolfe and the soldiers. Brendan and John approached the edge of the circle to see what would happen.

"Your time is ended, rough fool," Wolfe shouted. "You and the old patriarch will trouble Israel no more." Elijah stopped speaking and turned toward Wolfe.

"The wind is in the west, Elijah," Enoch said quietly. The sun still shone in the east, but dark clouds, rain clouds, grew above the western horizon.

Wolfe turned to the commander of his guard. "Kill them. Now."

"My Lord," questioned the commander, "what of the fire?"

"What of the fire?" Wolfe mocked him. The commander was caught between two lethal powers and seemed paralyzed, unable to choose. None of his men moved either. Mason Wolfe walked to the nearest soldier. "Give me your weapon." Wolfe took the assault rifle and surprised the commander by his familiarity with the mechanism. Wolfe set the weapon on full automatic, checked that the safety was off and raised the barrel. Old Enoch crumpled with the first burst of fire. Elijah stood resolutely as a second and longer burst killed him instantly. Wolfe returned the rifle to the soldier then turned back to the commander. "Now," he said as he pointed to Brendan and John at the edge of the crowd, "Arrest them."

Wolfe motioned to Scorfazza and they returned to the waiting limousine. Scorfazza felt a cool droplet and paused as he ducked to get inside the car. He held his hand up to the sky and said to Wolfe, "Rain, my Lord?" Wolfe nodded, looking pleased. And proud.

Mason Wolfe ordered that the bodies of Enoch and Elijah be left exposed at the place where they fell. A worldwide celebration was declared to mark the end of the drought and the end of those accursed prophets who had brought it. Wolfe declared "a new Christmas" and all around the world people unpacked old decorations and trees and lights. The store shelves were cleaned with a spontaneous renewal of the old gift-giving traditions.

Once again, Mason Wolfe had shown men everywhere why he ruled the earth. The rebellious nations seemed to respond to his political overtures and agreed to re-open peaceful discussions. Even so, Arab armies retained their ominous perches on Israel's borders. If Wolfe did not make good, they could still be at war within minutes. He determined to move quickly and ruthlessly to consolidate his gains.

It was only hours after Brendan's arrest that GDA troops stormed into Mrs. Habash's house in the Muslim section of old Jerusalem. They were surprised to find every person on their list sitting around the table in the main room and singing hymns after finishing a midday meal. It seemed that each of them, Michael Bern, Tom Bertoldi, the monk David, Mrs. Habash and the boy were waiting for the soldiers. The soldiers removed their prisoners and then searched the house. The communications room was dismantled. Wolfe had long ago cut off electrical power to the house, and so the soldiers were surprised to find no generator or other power source in the house. Likewise, the refrigerator was bare and without power.

It was the third day after Wolfe had personally murdered the two prophets and now he planned to crown the three days of celebrations with a final public execution. The guillotine was set up near the martyrs' bodies and as the time drew near, bloody-minded Jerusalemites made plans to attend. There would be no one clamoring to hear Elijah's teaching; only taunts and jeers for the Catholic pope.

"It has been three days since we were put into this hole," John observed. "Do you suppose the angel will free us one more time?"

From across the straw-strewn cell, Brendan assured him: "There will be no angel, John. Our work is ended. We will not wait long."

The soldiers came down at noon to prepare the prisoners. Brendan started to stand, but the first soldier into the cell clubbed him in the head. He fell backwards as the second soldier sprayed both him and John with pepper mace spray. Blinded now, and with their eyes and throats burning, they lay on the floor as the soldiers kicked them repeatedly in their heads and bodies. When the soldiers finished, they handcuffed each prisoner behind his back, shackled their legs and chained arms and legs together behind them. The prisoners could do nothing but lie on their sides or stomachs. The soldiers lifted them up by the arms and dragged them to a waiting van for the trip to the temple.

Mason Wolfe's entourage arrived at the temple ahead of the prisoners. As always, the television cameras would broadcast Wolfe's remarks. The execution of Brendan Shea was scheduled to follow.

Wolfe stepped onto the platform and walked to the microphone. The assembled mob cheered and hooted. They were not in a mood for speeches, but rather for blood. On the television, a long camera shot took in the grisly setting. On the left of the platform stood Wolfe at the podium. On the right half of the platform rose the guillotine and below on the pavement, in front of the platform, lay the bodies of Enoch and Elijah surrounded by four sentries.

"Brothers and Sisters, our long global nightmare is over," Wolfe began. "We have survived the most devastating, monstrous reign of terror in the history of humankind and three days ago that terror came to an end. And so I stand before you today in the presence of what remains of that vile era." Wolfe motioned toward the two bodies before him as he continued. "Before we finish today Brendan Shea and his henchmen will join them . . . ."

Wolfe felt a shaking and he paused. The quake grew stronger and the people became apprehensive. Earthquakes had happened here before and the firm rock of the temple mount—Wolfe knew—would not open beneath them. As the trembling grew more intense, there came another movement that made them all, including Wolfe, to seize with fear.

The four sentries noticed it first. Then there were shrieks from the front ranks of the spectators. By the time Enoch sat up, the cameras were fixed on the awakened prophets. Enoch and Elijah stood and turned to face Wolfe. The stunned guards were stiff with fright. Then saying nothing the two martyrs rose into the air and vanished amid the clouds while the whole world watched on television.

All along the borders of Israel, the hostile governments issued mobilization orders: the Syrians and Russians from the north, the Egyptians, Saudis and Libyans in the south, and the Jordanian/Iraqi coalition to the east. All the armies moved at once. Fighter/bomber aircraft launched for targets a mere ten minutes distant.

Finally the shaking stopped. As Wolfe had judged, the temple mount was spared damage and injury, even though much of the city had not. Wolfe was still recovering his wits when Brendan Shea and John Daniels were carried onto the platform bruised and bleeding. Their captors deposited them roughly in a kneeling position between Wolfe and the guillotine. The crowd jeered.

"Friends, do not fear. What you have seen was a trick, an illusion. I assure you those two criminals will never again darken the life of this planet. They are gone. Finished. But what is not finished is our day's work. Behold Brendan Shea, mass murderer and rebel! Beside him his chief minister, John Daniels, mass murderer and rebel! Both condemned to death. Wolfe nodded to two hooded men who had joined him on the platform.

Taking hold of John, they dragged him to the guillotine, for he was so shackled that he could not otherwise move. John made no sound as his lips moved in praise of God. He waited for his release. Wolfe came up beside Brendan who was bent low with a prayer that John would have strength. Then the beast-man crouched down next to the Vicar of Christ and lifted Brendan's chin so that their eyes met one last time. "It's over Brendan Shea. I have won." Wolfe grasped Brendan by the hair and yanked his head up to look at John and the machine. Then came the scrape and glint of the blade and John Daniels was gone.

Seconds later there came a bright flash from the northwest. It was like lightning. Then there was another to the north; and one closer toward the west until the eye could not count the flashes. From each brilliant flash there came a mushroom cloud that grew upward from the horizon and made everyone understand that war had come. Only Mason Wolfe's will and presence could have held the crowd back from chaos throughout the earthquake and the prophets' resurrection, but now the temple area was a complete confusion. The guards scattered with the people. Even Scorfazza disappeared in the turmoil.

Alone now, Wolfe dragged Brendan to the machine himself, all the while screaming for the executioners to pull John's body out of the thing. But no one was listening to the Lord of the World as the thermonuclear clouds multiplied over Israel's valley of Armageddon. Wolfe heaved the corpse aside himself and raised the blade. The whole world was coming undone, but no one bothered to watch as Mason Wolfe struggled to get Brendan into position. Brendan tried to co-operate, but with hands and legs trussed together he could do little but lay his head down once the madman had hauled him into position. Then Wolfe tripped the cord.

The blade had not traversed more than half its journey when it stopped. Brendan turned his head enough to see a particular nuclear cloud as it opened not many miles distant. What he saw was its rolling cap, utterly, peacefully still. Everywhere splitting atoms were suddenly frozen in mid-fission as time stopped and eternity began. Then Brendan heard the trumpet.

The End

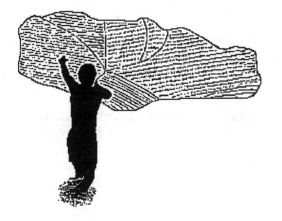

ORDER FORM: *THE LAST FISHERMAN*

Please send _____ copies of *The Last Fisherman*
by Randy England to:

Name _____ (print)

Street _____ (print)

City/State/Zip _____ (print)

$11.95 per copy. Add 7.225% sales tax to books shipped to Missouri addresses. Shipping: $2.95 for first book. Add $1.00 for each additional book. Mail check or money order to:

Convent Hill Publishing
1913 Cherry Street
Mexico, Missouri, 65265

Volume discounts available. Email: info@conventhill.com. For credit card sales go to our website at www.conventhill.com

ORDER FORM: *THE LAST FISHERMAN*

Please send _____ copies of *The Last Fisherman*
by Randy England to:

Name _____ (print)

Street _____ (print)

City/State/Zip _____ (print)

$11.95 per copy. Add 7.225% sales tax to books shipped to Missouri addresses. Shipping: $2.95 for first book. Add $1.00 for each additional book. Mail check or money order to:

Convent Hill Publishing
1913 Cherry Street
Mexico, Missouri, 65265

Volume discounts available. Email: info@conventhill.com. For credit card sales go to our website at www.conventhill.com

ORDER FORM: *THE LAST FISHERMAN*

Please send _____ copies of *The Last Fisherman*
by Randy England to:

Name _____ (print)

Street _____ (print)

City/State/Zip _____ (print)

$11.95 per copy. Add 7.225% sales tax to books shipped to Missouri addresses. Shipping: $2.95 for first book. Add $1.00 for each additional book. Mail check or money order to:

Convent Hill Publishing
1913 Cherry Street
Mexico, Missouri, 65265

Volume discounts available. Email: info@conventhill.com. For credit card sales go to our website at www.conventhill.com

---

ORDER FORM: *THE LAST FISHERMAN*

Please send _____ copies of *The Last Fisherman*
by Randy England to:

Name _____ (print)

Street _____ (print)

City/State/Zip _____ (print)

$11.95 per copy. Add 7.225% sales tax to books shipped to Missouri addresses. Shipping: $2.95 for first book. Add $1.00 for each additional book. Mail check or money order to:

Convent Hill Publishing
1913 Cherry Street
Mexico, Missouri, 65265

Volume discounts available. Email: info@conventhill.com. For credit card sales go to our website at www.conventhill.com